THE CRUISE OF THE

Santa Maria

Other books by the same author

THE CRUISE OF THE
Santa Maria

By EILÍS DILLON

Illustrated by Richard Kennedy

FUNK & WAGNALLS

A Division of Reader's Digest Books, Inc., New York

(1)

1420659

When we took the *Santa Maria* out for her first sail, we had
no idea that it was going to be such a long one, nor that it
would be so many weeks before we would see the rocky
shores of Connemara again.

She had a strange history, that boat. Perhaps this was why
we felt, even while we were pulling out from the pier, watching our neighbors waving to us and calling Godspeed, that
she was made for great deeds and high adventures like the
ones that people used to have in the old stories. I know that I
felt a long shudder run through me as we watched the land
fade from green to gray, until it disappeared altogether and
we were left alone on the dark-blue ocean.

The *Santa Maria* was begun by my grandfather when he
was almost sixty years old. She was a hooker, no different in
line, you would think, from any of the dozen that can be seen
every day lying against our quay wall. But there were differ-
ences. My grandfather had sailed in hookers since he was a
boy and he had a grudge against every boat that he had ever
traveled in. The *Santa Maria* was to be perfect. Every defect
in every hooker built since the beginning of time was to be
corrected in her.

Naturally, when he laid her keel in front of his own door,
all the men were willing to give him a hand with the build-

ing. My grandfather's house stood where it does still—only fifty yards from the quay of Rossmore. This meant that whenever a man was passing by to go to his own boat, he could drop in and see how the work was going on.

"Hoy, old Tom!" they would call out. "How is she shaping?"

Even then he was known as old Tom, perhaps because his wife had died a few years before. His daughter Maggie lived with him—a big, silent, red-haired woman, as strong as many a man, and as good to handle a boat as her father.

"She's shaping fine," my grandfather would say. "She's going to be the best hooker ever to come out of Rossmore."

At first no one minded this. They thought it was just his enthusiasm for the beginning of the building; and as any man who has ever built a boat knows, the first days of it are likely to drive you crazy with excitement.

But as the days and the weeks passed, one by one the men stopped calling out as they went by. The reason was simple. My grandfather had not stopped at saying that this would be the finest hooker. He had gone on to describe exactly what was wrong with his neighbors' hookers until he had insulted every boat in the whole district.

Rossmore is so called because it is the biggest promontory in our part of Connemara. It is really almost an island, connected to the shore by a narrow neck of land with a windy road on it. At the tip of Rossmore there is a little natural harbor. There our boats lie snug in the worst of weathers. We have a man-made pier—made in the time of the great Famine, they say. We have easy access to the open sea, not like the people of Rosmuc who have to sail under bridges and around reefs before they reach it. Our hookers are famous all over Connemara for their fine design, for their speed, and for the length of their lives.

I was a small boy, running unnoticed between the legs of my elders, when I heard them grumble to each other:

"Old Tom thinks he has a mission from heaven, to improve on all our work."

"He thinks he can do perfect work. Sure, don't we all know it's only God that works perfectly?"

"The things he said about my good boat!"

"And mine!"

"And mine, that has carried three generations in safety!"

"Do you think maybe he's a bit touched, for the want of his wife?"

This was Pat Conneeley, who always tried to make excuses for everyone.

"I wouldn't say that," said Michael Folan, who was my grandfather's nearest neighbor. "Hasn't he got Maggie, that's as good as any wife and has a lot less to say?"

Some of the men chuckled. To the day of her death, my grandmother had had the name of being the biggest talker from here to Galway. It was said of her that when she had no one else to talk to, she would go out and talk to the hens and chickens in the yard. Perhaps this was why Maggie was so silent, I thought. There could not be two talkers in the one house, the people always said.

"Whatever way it is," said Long Mike, "I can't make myself go and help that man any more. I know 'tisn't Christian. I know I should be in there a few days a week when I'd have the time, the way you'd do for any neighbor. But some day, if I had to listen to what he has to say about my boat, that's served me well for twenty-seven years, and my father before me for as many years more——"

He stuttered with fury. Michael Folan said:

"Sure, there's no sense in getting cross about it. That's how I am myself. Some day I'd be afraid I'd pick up a plank of wood and lay him out with it, when he'd be after insulting my good boat. And that would be less Christian than leaving him to it."

Being peaceful people, they left him alone, but sometimes when there was a wedding, or sports, or horse racing, and the men would have a drop to drink, they would let their anger show. If my grandfather were in the company, they would shout and call out to him above the heads of the people:

"How is the ark getting on? When will the flood be coming?"

Always someone with sense intervened then and got the shouter away so that the crossness never came to blows. All the same, over the years a bitterness grew up until everyone for miles around had heard of the perfect hooker. I did not know whether to be ashamed or proud of it. My father spoke to me of it:

"Sometimes it happens that a kind of demon gets into a man so that he must set to and do a certain thing, even if it seems mad to everyone else. It's that demon that sends a man away from his family and his warm hearth to explore in the Antarctic, with no company but the seals and the penguins. That's what it is with my father. He has to build that boat, until the demon goes out of him. Otherwise he would never sleep, never eat, nor have a moment's peace of mind."

This made sense to me.

Then, when the hooker was almost finished, the old man died. That was when I was fifteen years old, a year before my story begins. I had become rather friendly with my grandfather by then, though he hardly ever spoke to me. I used to go sometimes and watch him at work on the boat, marveling at how he could content himself to go so slowly. He was just turned seventy when he died, and a little shake in his hands perhaps foretold that he was near his end. It annoyed him to see his hands shake and sometimes, very rarely, he would let me drive a nail or two for him, but only after he had put them in position. He was planking the little foredeck just before he became too ill to work any more.

One day I came running in home to tell my mother that he had fallen and that Maggie had got him to bed. My mother sent me running again, to fetch the priest. That was a slow business—all the way up to the mainland and along the longest mile of ground in the world. By the time I got back, riding pillion behind the priest, the old man was nearly finished.

When the priest had gone away again, I came fearfully into the little bedroom to see if my mother needed me. Maggie was there, with the tears running unheeded down her face.

"John, he's asking for you. Go over to him quick or it will be too late. Hurry."

She pushed me over to the bed where the old man lay. I found suddenly that I was not frightened at all. He had not changed much, except that I had never seen him so pale before.

"John. The boat." His words came with difficulty. "Her name. *Santa Maria*. You'll sail her. First. You'll be the first. *Santa Maria*. Not an Irish name. They don't deserve it. *Santa Maria*." He looked at me, suddenly sharp. "You'll sail her."

"Yes, yes, I'll sail her," I said in a low voice. "And her name will be *Santa Maria*."

Then he closed his eyes without a word of thanks and my mother signaled to me that I could go. That same evening she told me that he was dead.

By the time the funeral was over, everyone knew that the boat was to be my responsibility and my inheritance. Naturally everyone was interested, but my grandfather's hooker had been such a source of contention for so long that no one liked to ask any questions about it. Michael Folan, whose son Jim was my great friend, came all the way up the hill to our house a week after my grandfather died and sat in the kitchen for an hour before he could bring the conversation around to the hooker. My father was there because it was a Sunday morning. It was a fine day in March, I remember well—one of those spring days that make you think that summer may really come after all. A wide bar of sunlight lay on the kitchen floor, with our cat settled in the middle of it, as warm as if she had been in front of the fire.

Michael said:

"Ah, he was a great man, your father. Headstrong too, like many a good man before him. What will you do with the new boat?"

Now that he had got the question out, his eyes danced with curiosity for the answer.

"She's not finished yet," my father said.

"You won't want for helpers to finish her," Michael said eagerly. "It was the way your father turned the helpers away. Now that he's gone where we'll all be going someday, with the help of God, we can tell you that you have only to ask and you'll have ten hands at your disposal——"

"Thanks, Michael," my father said. "I don't doubt it. But my sister Maggie says she's going to finish it herself."

"Maggie!"

"Yes. She said it the day of the funeral. You know Maggie doesn't have much to say at the best of times."

"Aye, she's a quiet one."

"Well, that day she didn't say much either, only that she had promised her father that she would finish the boat."

"Maybe we'll never see that hooker take to the water," said Michael.

He was bitterly disappointed, as we could see. It was clear that the whole of Rossmore was longing for the day when the truth of my grandfather's boasting would be put to the proof. I don't say that they were hoping she would lie over on her side immediately and sink. However, they wouldn't be people at all, but saints, if they did not hope that the hooker would show a list, at the very least.

"Maggie won't be so slow," my father said with his usual good-humored smile, though he could guess at Michael's thoughts as well as I did. "She doesn't waste time in talking, for one thing."

"She does not, faith," said Michael. "Tell her anyway that we'll all be glad to help her and advise her if she needs it. She has only to say the word."

Maggie never said that word. With her own two hands she finished the hooker, planking it and caulking it, early and late. She was not slow, either. Less than three months after my grandfather's death, the hooker was finished.

By that time, the men had developed the habit of leaning on the stone wall by Maggie's house to watch her at work. She did not seem to mind, though I would have thought that the row of silent watchers would have worn her nerves down. They were friendly, which was probably why she did not object to them. Also, as each man came along he always called out, as they used to do at first to her father:

"Hoy, Maggie! How is she shaping?"

Maggie would lift her right hand and say one word to each of them:

"Well."

That was all. Gradually the men developed a great respect for her. More than once I heard them say:

"Someone lost a great wife in Maggie."

Then, one evening, they could see by the way she was walking around and around the hooker that there was no more to be done. Long Mike said:

"She's finished."

"She is," said Maggie.

"But for the mast," Long Mike said. "You'll need help to launch her and to step the mast."

"I will," said Maggie.

Several of the men walked over to take a close look, for the first time, at the work of more than ten years. Jim and I were there, and several other boys of our age who had almost come to believe that the tarpaulin-covered carcass of the great hooker was as natural to the scene as a rock or a tree. There was something shocking in the thought that it was going to be moved.

"Before we launch her, she'll need a few coats of tar," Michael Folan said. "I'll bring you down some in the morning——"

"No!" Maggie said it so fiercely that the men dropped their hands, which had been stroking and fondling the boat. "She's to be painted, Father said, blue below the waterline, red and blue above." She looked at them desperately. "He said it, nearly the last thing, before he died. How can I go against him?"

"Paint will do fine. Why should you go against him? Aren't half the boats in the world painted?"

These things the men said, though it was easy to see that they thought this was the final evidence that old Tom had been a bit soft before the end. Tar was the thing for hookers, they all knew. To use paint seemed like an insult to every hooker that ever sailed out from Connemara.

Maggie had to make a trip to Galway for special paint. She went on Long Mike's boat when he was taking in some lambs to the July fair, and he said she never spoke a word the whole way there and back. She brought great tins of paint, and brushes, and laid them all out on the floor by the kitchen dresser. I saw them at once, the day after she came back when I went to visit her.

"Maggie," I said, "won't you let me help with the painting?"

She looked at me strangely for a full minute so that I thought she was going to make no reply. Then I saw that she was working her hands around and around as if she were making bread, catching them and squeezing them in an agony of nervous fear.

"I'd like it," she said at last. "I'd like it fine. But he said I was to finish it myself. He said no one else but him and me was to put a hand to the building of that boat."

"This is not building," I said quickly. "You finished the building yourself."

"I did, God help me, and I knowing all my neighbors were laughing to see a woman at such work."

"They were not laughing. They were admiring your skill. Many a man I heard say he wished he could work like you."

She looked at me doubtfully and I was afraid she would go silent again. In all my life I had never had such a long conversation with her.

"This is not building," I said again. "This is painting. He wouldn't mind your having help with the painting. Sure, won't she have to be painted every year of her life? He must have known well that you couldn't paint her every year as long as she lasts. She'll last a hundred years."

"I'd like a bit of help with the painting, sure enough," she said after a long pause.

So the very next day we started, early in the morning, and for more than a month I used to go down when I'd have time to spare, and sandpaper and paint with Maggie. She would never let me work on the boat alone. Always while I worked on one part, she worked on another, as if to make herself feel that she was keeping the charge her father had given her.

I was very glad of this, because before the painting was finished Maggie had become almost talkative. It was true she never talked of anything but our work. She would make tea, exactly halfway through the time we had allotted for the day's painting, and while we drank it she would always try to estimate how much was left to be done.

"Five coats she must have, over every inch, and an extra one if the wood swallows the paint. That's what he said."

Then one day she added with a little chuckle: "He would have taken ten years more to finish that, God help us."

This was the first time she had ever dared to show anything but the most intense respect for her father's plan. I began to think she would be glad when that hooker would be gone from before her front door and she could give her time to keeping her house and her pigs and her chickens, surely a more natural life for a woman.

The day of the launching she was as nervous as a hen with chickens. She could take no part at all in this and it was obvious that she hated to see the men handling the boat, getting it on the rollers, taking it down to the beach, shouting directions to each other as if they thought it was just an ordinary hooker. Indeed they seemed to have forgotten whose boat it was, in the excitement. Fortunately Maggie went silent, so they could not tell what thoughts were burning in her brain. Now that I knew her better I could guess at them a little. Michael Folan bawled out:

"Give her a kick there in the bows! Do you want her to fly off the rollers?"

I saw Maggie go red with anger. Later, at the tricky moment when the hooker took to the water, they called her names that they would use to a cow or a mare that would be obstreperous. Then Maggie clenched her hands and turned away up to her house. I went with her a piece of the way. She said:

"Tell them—tell them—to come up—when they have her afloat. I have a drop in the bottle for them. Tell them that. Oh, John," she said suddenly, " 'tis a terrible thing to be a woman! If I were a man, I'd sail the seven seas in that boat, yes, and I'd need no man's help to launch her. But to be a woman—and to have hair the color of mine as well——"

I could say nothing in answer to this. I knew what she meant. A red-haired woman, our people say, brings bad luck if you meet her on the way to the sea. That was why Maggie used to stay inside the house so much, because it was near the sea and the men had to pass by on their way to the boats. She said something of this to me now:

"How could I come to my door and call out to the men and they on their way out for a night's fishing, maybe, or over to Aran with a load of turf? If a storm blew up and they were drowned, I'd be blamed forever after."

It had never struck me before to think of this silly old superstition from her point of view. It worried me a good deal, and I determined to ask my father's opinion on it at the first opportunity. I could tell that Maggie loved the sea as much as her father had done. It seemed wrong that she should never be able to gratify her longing for it again. Only her father had had the courage to go to sea with her.

At her door, we turned and looked back. Now the men had the hooker moored. She sat as straight and firm as a swan, rising and falling on the gentle swell with a swan's easy grace.

"Look at that!" Maggie said in a low voice. "She's a good boat."

The men agreed on this later, as they sat in the kitchen sipping their poiteen and planning tomorrow's work of stepping the mast. It was lying ready on two trestles, at the gable of the house, well weathered.

"A young larch tree, the best mast you can have," said Michael Folan. "When the mast is up, she can be named."

"*Santa Maria* is her name," I said.

It was the first time I had mentioned it and I thought this a good moment when the men were in good humor after launching the boat and with the glasses in their hands. Instantly their faces darkened.

"What nonsense is this?"

"Why should she have a foreign name?"

"Isn't there an Irish saint good enough for her, and we having saints in every townland, nearly?"

"My grandfather said it, just before he died."

I did not tell them that he had said he would not use the name of an Irish saint because his neighbors had disrespected his boat. It seemed to me that if they had that information, the hooker might go a long time without a mast.

"*Santa Maria* is a fine name," I said, calling up my courage. "It's the name of the mother of God. No one could say it's not a good name for a boat."

" 'Twould be a fine name if it were in Irish and not in Spanish."

Then they stopped protesting. Pat Conneeley said gently: "God be merciful to the souls of the dead."

"Amen," said the rest of them, and I saw that for Maggie's sake they were prepared to forgive the old man his outlandish ideas.

So when the mast was fixed, the name was painted on. I did that myself, leaning over her bows where she was tied against the quay. The white paint shone out handsomely against the dark blue, and I thought how much better she looked, how much cleaner and lighter than the rows of tarry boats that belonged to the people of Rossmore.

Maggie had made the great black sails with her own hands. They were finished more than a year before and she had laid them away in the huge press in her own room. She got them out on the day after the name was painted on the hooker and she said to me:

"John, it's time to think of sailing her. When will you go?"

"As soon as I can put sail on her."

"Do you know what they're saying?" Maggie asked me.

"Yes, I heard it."

"That that boat is made for misfortune. That she hasn't a right name but a foreign one. That she was partly built by a red-haired woman. That not a man of them would go on her outside the quay."

"I heard all that."

"Are you afraid?"

"No."

"Why are you not afraid?"

"Because she sails high and free. Because she has the best name she could have. Because she was built by people that understand boats. It would be foolish and superstitious to be afraid of her."

"How will you find someone to sail with you?"

For one moment a wild notion flew into my mind that Maggie herself was the person who should come with me. If she had been a man, there would have been no doubt at all about it. But then I thought of the storm I would raise among our superstitious neighbors if it became known that I was to set out on this boat, which they already feared, with a red-haired woman. I could imagine the procession of sages that would appear one by one in our kitchen, foretelling disaster.

"I'll ask Jim Folan," I said. "He doesn't care about those old stories, no more than I do."

"Yes, Jim is a good sailor too, though he is so young. But hurry, because the summer is going from us."

There was a feel of autumn in the air, though it was only August. It showed in the darkening edges of the bramble leaves, in the long, dewy mornings, and in the fading watercress on the stream that ran down to the harbor. The days were warm, however, and the little corn that we grow was still standing in the fields. It was good sailing weather, with dark-blue sea and sky and not a cloud to be seen.

"We should go at once, without any delay," Jim said as soon as I asked him, "before the storms begin in September."

"Aren't you afraid of the *Santa Maria*, like everyone else?"

"Those are only pishrogues," said Jim with certainty. "It's silly, un-Christian talk."

"Do you think we'll believe in those pishrogues when we're old?"

"I don't know. Age does queer things to people. I don't believe in them now, anyway."

Boys are not as easily able to make their own arrangements in Rossmore as I believe they do in other parts of the world. I had no difficulty in persuading my father to let me go. Though he was uneasy, he felt that he had to agree because it was his father who had asked for it. But my mother had been affected by the talk of the women, who had already begun to warn her. Every day when she went to the well for water, she said, some old granny would call out that she would be praying for my safety when I'd go in that terrible hooker. Still, my mother said that if my father agreed, she would make no objection.

Jim's mother was harder to convert. His father was a fine sailor and he had faith in Jim.

"Didn't I teach him myself to handle a hooker?" he said. "There's nothing he doesn't know about boats—he's as knowledgeable as myself. Do you want to make a mollycoddle of him?"

"I want to make old bones of him," his mother said; "after all the work I put into rearing him, I want to have the satisfaction of seeing him a man."

Jim told me afterwards that this talk nearly stopped him from coming with me, not because he was afraid but because of his mother's fears. However, after a long discussion, she agreed that I could not go alone, that my father could not come with me because if the hooker were really doomed this would leave my mother with no one to fend for her, and that charity demanded that she sacrifice her Jim. All of this I heard much later. Indeed it is doubtful how long my own courage would have lasted if I had heard the gloomy talk that was going on. It is always thought to be unlucky to mention the possibility of misfortune in the presence of those who are likely to suffer it. People took trouble, therefore, to conceal some of these conversations from us.

Still we could see, on the morning we sailed out of the harbor, that there was a feeling of excitement among the men who waved us out. My mother was there, and Jim's, but Maggie did not come down to the quay. I had been to visit her for a moment on my way to the boat.

"You'll bring her back safe, John," she said as I left her. "Then they can have no more talk of bad luck and misfortune."

She gave me a huge soda-cake and said an old blessing over me, so fast and low that I could not catch the words. She did not come to the door to watch me go.

So we left Rossmore quay with a feeling of high adventure, as I said, and never dreaming that it would be many weeks before we would see it again.

(2)

Sitting back in the stern of the hooker, handling the tiller, I was able for a long time, by turning my head a little, to see the white speck that was our house on the hill above the harbor. When that disappeared I was almost glad, for now we could give our full attention to the boat. We had all sail up and were clipping along before a following wind that seemed to have been sent specially to help us.

With bursting pride, I thought of my grandfather. This hooker was a wonder, a miracle. Never had I sailed in anything like her. She rode the waves like a sea gull, with hardly a splash, with hardly a creak of her timbers. The sea today was a challenge to her, with long, strong, gray-blue waves that would have sent any but the best of boats bumping about like an old barrel. Overhead a blue sky with scrappy white clouds gave a promise that this wind would not fail.

Jim came to sit with me.

"She'll sail herself," he said. "We could cross the Atlantic in her. We could sleep in her, and she'd find her own way."

A thought came to me, small and ridiculous at first but then growing and growing until I could no longer hold it back:

"It would take a while to cross the Atlantic. At the rate we're going, it wouldn't take long to sail to Aran."

"To Aran!"

"Did anyone ask you where we intended to go?"

"No one."

"No one asked me either, not even my father."

"I suppose no one thought it worthwhile asking. They would think we would just go along toward Carraroe, maybe, or even to Rossaveel, and then turn back when we'd be hungry."

"We won't be hungry," I said. "We have a mountain of food. And Maggie gave me that huge loaf and we just leaving."

"We might never get the chance again," Jim said. "A fair wind, plenty of food, and the blessing of all our neighbors and relations. I have a great longing on me to go to Aran."

"We could show them the boat. They don't build boats like this in Aran."

"We could show them what the Rossmore people can do."

"They never saw the like of this boat in all their lives."

So we went on, boasting and gloating, enjoying in advance the look of black envy that we knew would greet us as we would sail in triumph alongside the pier at Kilronan. We were so busy at it that we did not notice the sky and sea change color. Even a sudden sharpness in the wind did not wake us out of our dream. It was not until a few drops of rain splashed on our faces that we stopped and looked at each other in consternation. The dark-blue rolling sea was now a heavy gray, matching the huge, blackish cloud that hung like a sail over us. Beyond the cloud there was still blue sky to be seen, but even as we watched, this turned white and then gray. Heavy raindrops pitted the surface of the sea, which suddenly looked very deep and terrifying.

Without a word we went to work, taking down the mainsail, leaving only the little jib. Still the hooker plunged along, but she was quieter now. She rode the waves steadily, never lurching as I have seen hookers do in storms less fierce than this, and she never shipped as much as a drop of water.

The screaming wind lifted the sea all around us into great steely hills and hollows. I remember wondering if birds feel fear during a storm, or if the ease of their wings gives them only a sensation of extra lightness, when the wind carries them along. Certainly this was how I felt now. In spite of the discomfort of our position I felt like shouting with the wind, urging it on to stronger and stronger force so that the boat would fly over the waves even faster. Since the sails were down, there was no doubting that boat. I knew that Jim felt the same trust in her when he said:

"My grandfather—my mother's father that sailed the Atlantic in the hooker with Captain Hennessy—he always said when he talked about it that the storms were hardly dangerous at all so long as you had no canvas up and were riding before it."

"So long as you have a good boat," I said.

"The main difference between us and those old fellows," said Jim after a moment, "is that they were prepared to sail a couple of thousand miles. I don't want to land up in America, if this storms lasts long enough."

"Neither do I."

There was no land to be seen, neither behind us nor before us, except where a little darkening of the horizon at one place might have been the smallest Aran island. The rain was heavy over there. Where we were, only an occasional shower came thundering down on us. Soon we were drenched to the skin. I said:

"Did your granddaddy happen to say how he dried his clothes after those storms?"

"In the sun, he said, when the storm was over."

"We'll have a long wait for the sun, I'm thinking."

Now the sky was black from side to side. Not a glimmer of light showed, not the smallest shaft of cold, sharp sunlight poking its way through to tell us that the storm would end sometime. All around us the sea reflected the black sky, except where the tops of the waves showed white like teeth. The *Santa Maria* felt very, very small. Still I did not distrust her. Jim said:

"They'll all be praying for us at home."

After that we were silent for a long time. We could both imagine the things that were being said at Rossmore, not only in our houses but in every house in the townland:

"They were warned not to go. 'Tis an unlucky boat. It couldn't have luck. Bad enough for a woman to have a hand in it, but a woman with red hair would be certain to make an end of it. A fine August day, not a cloud in the sky until they put to sea. 'Tis a terrible thing to go against nature, to go against tradition, to go against the old people that have the wisdom of the ages stored up in their heads."

This would be the signal for all the old grannies to burst into ologoning. I could nearly hear them, giving long wails out of them that would set all the dogs going in competition. Especially I could imagine how this would anger my mother, and how she would have to pretend that she had no fears for us. If she showed signs of anxiety, the old ones would redouble their howls.

There was nothing whatever that we could do, except to wait for the wind and the sea to bring us wherever they wanted. We got out some of our food, which was safe and dry in the lee of the cabin, in a strong canvas bag. The only way into the cabin of a hooker is through a hatchway in the deck above. If we had stored our food in there, we would have gone hungry—certainly neither of us would have chosen to climb up on the deck with that terrible wind clawing at us.

We found our courage had come back, after we had eaten. Still the hooker plunged along. It would be daylight for many hours yet, and we were thankful for this. Whatever hope we had of making land somewhere, without light it would be impossible. To my astonishment I began to feel sleepy, and with this came all sorts of visions to torment me— of a warm turf fire, and the smell of new bread, and the soft yellow light of an oil lamp, and worst of all, of my feather-bed in the room behind the kitchen where I always slept.

Then we saw the island. It was away down on our left, not in the direction of the Aran islands at all. We knew that these must still be straight in front of us, and we were so busy watching for them to appear through the rain clouds that we had failed to see the other island until it was a clear gray line no more than a mile or two away.

"Is it Lettermore, or Lettermullen?" Jim wondered. "If it's one of those we're in luck. We'll have word back to Ross-more by the telegraph in no time, saying we're safe."

"Both of those islands have bridges to the mainland," I said after a moment. "That one is much farther out. I don't think I ever saw it before."

"Of course you saw it. Isn't it on the way in to Galway? You must have seen it."

By the note of fright in his voice I guessed that the same thought was in his mind as was in my own, one that I would have been ashamed to express. This was that the strange island could possibly be that ghostly island which they say sometimes rises out of the sea, to entice sailors to land. It is a favorite story of the old people, that on that island no one ever grows old, no one ever does wrong, wonderful flowers and trees bloom all the year round, wonderful birds fly about and settle on your hands when you call them. The only draw-back is that once you land there, you cannot leave again. Some people who managed to escape came home to their own place to find all their relations dead and gone, and strange faces all around them, because what had seemed like a short stay on the Island of the Young was really a hundred years.

The stories about the enchanted island were many, but on one point they were all agreed: that if you were doomed to land there, no power on earth could prevent it. Your boat would be borne along by water spirits and driven up on the shores of the island, no matter how you might try to keep off. During the next hours, this was certainly what seemed to be happening to the *Santa Maria*. Of course I did not believe in those old stories now, but from time to time it seemed that I returned suddenly, for a terrifying second, to the age when I had sat in a long skirt on a tiny creepie stool by our fire at home, listening to an old man from the mountain tell of people he had known who had been carried off to the Land of Youth. A great wind came and blew their boats, he said, from wave to wave of the ocean, until it landed them on the enchanted shores where it never rained, and where the sun always shone.

Long before we landed on that strange island, we had one positive proof that it was not the enchanted one. The rain fell on it in torrents, in great streams that looked as if they would end by washing every blade of grass off it into the sea. Indeed it did not look that day as if many blades of grass grew on it, even in the best of weathers. It was the most desolate place I have ever seen. The part we could see was surrounded by yards of huge, murderous-looking rocks, blackened and battered by the sea so that they did not seem able to support even a few shreds of seaweed. The tide was high, and we could see reefs like long, black sea monsters reaching out for us as our boat plunged toward them.

I could almost have believed that some evil demons were carrying the *Santa Maria* along. The wind was stronger now than any time since we had set out. We were working in short tacks, in a desperate effort to save ourselves, but there was no withstanding that wind. It was the saddest moment of my life, I think, when we knew without any further doubt that the *Santa Maria* was going to strike.

It was Jim that saved her, though neither he nor anyone else could have kept her off that shore. He was at the tiller, because being a little bigger than I was, his arms were stronger. By some powerful instinct, in the one moment when the *Santa Maria* wavered in the shallower water, he steered her between two great, misshaped boulders. Beyond them, the rocks were a little smaller and more closely placed. Above them was a stony beach, over which the waves ran chasing each other, almost to the base of a little grass-topped cliff in which we could see the mouth of a cave.

We had no sooner passed between the two boulders than a great gust of wind came whistling and roaring between them after us. It caught the stern of the *Santa Maria* and lifted it bodily out of the water, and then crashed it down on the rocks with gigantic force.

For a long moment, it seemed as if the storm had suddenly ceased. The boat lay quietly, then rolled a little. I heard Jim's voice shouting:

"She's holed! Get ashore!"

I saw him seize the bag of food from which we had eaten sometime before, and then drop it again as he realized that it would be impossible to carry it. In a kind of daze I swung a leg over the side, where she had listed, and let myself down into the sea.

Immediately a monstrous wave knocked me flat. The water was not deep, but the rocks were wickedly painful to walk on with bare feet and the waves seemed like hands pulling at my ankles. I struggled upright and tried again, on all fours, sometimes able to walk two or three steps before falling. I swallowed mouthfuls of salty water, and felt my head spin with fatigue and with the sight of the whirling foam. I hardly knew whether Jim was alive or dead, until I felt him take my arm and heave me over the last few steps to safety.

Like old, old men, bent with years of labor in the fields, we plodded step by step as far from the sea as we could go. At the foot of the cliff, we stopped and turned without a word toward the cave.

It was cold as the grave in there, but it was sheltered a little at the back from the wind and the rain. Once we were inside, I felt relieved to be free of the noise of the storm.

Through the opening of the cave, we could see a part of my grandfather's wonderful boat. We did not look at each other. After a long time, Jim said:

"Pity we couldn't have brought some food from her."

It seemed to me that I would never want to move from that cave again, that I would sit there gazing at the wreck of the *Santa Maria* until I would turn into a pillar of stone like the villains in the old stories.

Perhaps I would have done this, if we had not heard the sound of feet running directly above our heads. It was an astonishing sound to us. The place had looked so desolate that I had imagined the whole island to be uninhabited. At first we could hardly tell whether they were human feet or the feet of some animal. They ran lightly, but with a kind of prancing rhythm that made me think of centaurs—those creatures that are half man and half horse. They were favorite characters in the old stories, though the storytellers always took the trouble to explain that they are only to be found in the islands of Greece.

Wild thoughts chased each other through my head, which was already shaken into a state of foolishness by the storm. I felt Jim pulling at my shoulder, saying in a hoarse whisper:

"Someone running! Can't you hear?"

"Yes."

"Well, come outside. We've got to lay claim to our boat before some blackguard says he salvaged her."

This roused me to life, you may be sure. I followed Jim out of the cave. Together we limped down to the sea's edge, until the foaming waves were washing around our toes. There was no sign of the runner. Whoever it was would have to go along a piece of the cliff, before finding a place where he could climb down onto the shore.

Then we saw him, scrambling down a rough path from the cliff above, sending the loose stones rattling and rolling before him. He came on quite confidently, as if he knew every step. Gradually Jim and I moved together, almost as if we needed to protect each other. Yet this poor creature could hardly have injured anyone. Though he moved with such agility, we could see that he was very old, and he was so thin and worn that either of us could have knocked him down with a push of the shoulder if we had had a mind to. But there was something unearthly about him, something wild and strange, that made us think of that other terrible story of an island inhabited by a solitary old man who makes slaves of castaway sailors and keeps them there until they die of despair.

When he came to the place where we stood side by side at the sea's edge, the old man did not stop nor seem to notice

us at all. He ran straight into the sea, staggering through the waves, seeming to care nothing that he was being soaked through his rags to the skin, until he reached the hooker. Still we stood and watched him, while he stroked her with his hands as if she had been a horse. Her name seemed specially to fascinate him. He ran his fingers around the letters, tracing them as if he were writing them newly, while the waves roared waist high around him.

Then suddenly he was plunging back to the sea's edge again. When he reached us, he stood and stared from one of us to the other as if he were hoping to recognize us. His actions were so strange, and his whole appearance so wild that our first thought was that he was crazy. But when we looked into his eyes, they were as sane as our own. They looked hungry, lonely, anxious, miserable, but they did not look mad.

Neither did he sound mad when he spoke. Indeed we could hardly hear what he said at first. His voice was low and rather hoarse, as if he did not use it much. Besides his first words were so unexpected that we could not make sense of them at all.

"You come from Sarah," he said. "You don't look Spanish."

Some instinct warned us not to tell him brutally that we did not understand him. He looked so anxiously at us that it would have seemed cruel to have answered him carelessly.

"We are not Spanish," I said gently.

He pulled us by an arm each along the shore toward the little path by which he had descended.

"But you have the *Santa Maria*. Oh, she's a beauty. I always heard she was a beauty." He looked quickly from one of us to the other. "She's holed, but we'll fix her, easy. We can't touch her till the storm dies down. She's safe in there, behind the rocks. Up to my house and you'll tell me all about your voyage. It will be long telling. And about Sarah. You'll tell me about Sarah. She was a beauty. Oh, she was a beauty too.

But now she's so much older. Tell me, is she a beauty still?"

"Yes," I said.

"Ah! Women do be beauties too, at her age. Tell me now, are ye hungry?"

"We are, and cold," said Jim. "Have you a fire above in your place?"

"A grand fire. I haven't much else, but I always have a grand fire."

He skipped up the cliff path before us. We followed more slowly, feeling every step in our bare feet. The wind did its best to push us off the path, catching us in a kind of whirl where it struck the cliff's face. When we reached the top, it was a different wind, a great roaring giant that would have lifted us in its huge arms and dashed us down onto the beach, if we had not clung together.

"Down, down, like the old fellow!" Jim bawled into my ear.

Sure enough, he was running away ahead of us, going like an old crab—flat, with splayed-out arms and legs as if to grip the ground with claws. We crouched down, and found the going easier. Almost crawling, we followed him down from the highest point of the little cliff until we felt the force of the wind lighten a little. Then we stood upright and looked around us.

Away off below us, a long grassy plain stretched down into but we could make out by the roll of the land that there was a valley and up again to a low hill. All around us was the sea, more of the island below the hill. The old man was standing up now. He was quite tall and straight. He turned and saw that we had paused, and he waved us forward with an impatient hand. We hurried after him, down across the valley. It was covered with thin grass, growing on sand, as we could see now. Perhaps one could graze a few sheep there but it would have been a poor pasture. Rabbit burrows were everywhere, looking dismal now with the rain soaking the sandy passageways that led into them. It was a lonely, desolate place. The wind drove the rain in heavy sweeps across it.

Somehow it seemed colder now, worse than it had been on the shore. We crossed the valley and climbed the hill at the opposite side. Here the grass was full of sea-pinks in full bloom. They reminded me suddenly that this was still the summer. Indeed on a good summer's day it would have been beautiful, with larks singing and the blue sea all around. Still the old man kept ahead of us. Jim said:

"He seemed to be expecting us. Who is Sarah, I wonder?"

"Heaven knows," I said. "We'll find out as we talk to him, perhaps."

"Do you think he's daft?"

"No. Maybe with a bit of luck we'll meet someone on the way to his house that will be able to tell us about him, and maybe even tell us who Sarah is."

But a minute later we reached the top of the hill and saw the rest of the island.

"I don't think we'll meet anyone else," Jim said.

Down from us, the sandy grass ran a piece of the way, and then there were a few real fields. We could see potatoes growing and two small fields of wheat. The darker fields beyond them looked like barley. Between these fields a little road wriggled along to the door of a low, thatched house. The thatch was new and clean and the walls of the house were whitewashed. Smoke came up from the chimney in a thick stream. It was a comfortable little scene, except for one thing. In all the island, so far as we could see, there was only that one house.

"We're lucky to find a house at all," Jim said. "There must have been plenty of families here at one time."

Sure enough, now that we had paused to examine the landscape, we could see here and there the ruins of many little houses. They were a familiar sight to us, because they were the same as those that can be seen all over Connemara.

Four stone walls with stone chimneys stood solidly against the weather. To live in one of them, one would only need to lay a thatched roof on top. From every one of them a family had set out for America, leaving the thatch to fall in and the nettles and briars to crowd against the walls. In the bad old times in Ireland this happened so often that some of the islands and even some districts on the mainland lost their whole population.

On this island, we thought, the wonder was that one family had stayed. The grassy hill over which we had come sheltered the land a little from the worst of the Atlantic storms. But for many months of the year the wind and the rain would possess that island completely. The thought of living there filled me with despair.

By the time we reached the door of the house, the old man had gone inside. The front yard was clean and free of weeds, and a little rose tree, with water-logged roses, trailed against the whitewashed wall. At one end of the house, in a lean-to shed, a few hens clustered miserably from the rain.

Naturally all of this led us to expect that we would find a whole family in the kitchen before us. There was no one, no one at all except the old man on his knees before the fire, reddening it into a blaze with fresh sods of turf. He took these from the little pile that stood against the wall—strong, dry, black turf. It warmed up the whole room, and sent a glow through every part of us as only a turf fire can do. Its light shone on a big dresser full of rosy cups and plates, luster jugs and vases, all clean and gleaming. There was a settle bed against one wall, a table under the window, and a few chairs and stools which looked very old and worn. A mother cat and two half-grown kittens occupied one of the hobs. The old man pulled a creaky chair in front of the fire for each of us.

"Sit in there now and warm your shins while I make a cup of tea." He cocked a sharp eye, like a bird's, at us. "Oh, yes,

I have tea. Great stuff to warm you up, especially with a drop of something else in it."

"Are you alone in the house?" Jim asked suddenly.

"Yes, and alone on this island, except when I have visitors like yourselves, and that doesn't happen often. I'm a good housekeeper, as you can see."

"There's no doubt that you are," I said. "Inside and out, you'd think this house had two women looking after it."

He gave a happy little cackle of laughter.

"I keep it exactly as she did," he said.

"As who did?"

"Sarah, of course."

He filled a little black kettle from a can of water and hung it on the crane over the fire. Within a few minutes it was singing, the sweetest sound in the world. While the water was heating, he was getting out three ancient, cracked mugs, though there were plenty of china cups on the dresser. Then he fetched a loaf of soda-bread from the press below.

"I'm not a bad hand at the bread," he said, "but I have no butter. I have only the goats since my cow died. You'd have a job to get an ounce of butter from a goat. Sometimes I get butter when I go over to Garraroe on a fine day. I finished the last of it yesterday. I have goat's milk for the tea, though."

He chatted excitedly like this all the time, while he made the tea and cut the bread with an ancient, bone-handled knife. His brown teapot had lost most of its spout, but the tea came out good and strong. Into each cup he poured a few drops of poiteen, saying to us as he did so:

"I don't hold with boys tasting poiteen, unless they have just been shipwrecked. Drink up now, let you, and eat plenty of bread."

The bread was reasonably good, as he had boasted, though for want of some butter it did not taste anything like my mother's bread. Still we worked steadily at it, and every time we showed signs of slackening, he pushed more slices toward

35

us, watching us delightedly all the time. Throughout the meal, we kept glancing at each other, hopelessly trying to pick up inspiration. By the time we had finished, each of us had become so anxious to avoid the other's eyes that we were both staring at our toes.

When it was plain that we could eat no more, the old man said:

"Now we can sit by the fire as long as we like. That rain won't leave off for the rest of the day."

"The *Santa Maria*——" I said.

"She'll be safe enough. The wind is gone down." He looked eagerly from one of us to the other and said: "I'm a man of patience. Now you have eaten well. I waited until you were finished. Now you can tell me all about Sarah."

(3)

This time, there was no escape. The old man's anxious, un-happy eyes were fixed on us, hungry for the news that he thought we could give. It was clear that only heroic devotion to the laws of hospitality had prevented him from question-ing us before now. After a pause, I said gently:

"I'm afraid you are mistaken. We don't know Sarah at all. We don't even know who she is."

"But you came on the *Santa Maria.*" He looked wildly from me to Jim and back again, and said accusingly: "The *Santa Maria* came straight to the shore below, to the very spot she sailed from twenty years ago." He hitched his chair so close that his ragged, bony knee was pushed hard against mine. "I was sitting here by the fire, thinking I wouldn't go out until the rain would leave off, thinking it was a queer time of the year for a storm to come up. Then I began to remember that other storm in August, twenty years ago this year, when Sarah went away on the *Santa Maria.* I had the fire going nicely and I was just thinking I'd get down a book and have a bit of reading for myself. Then a feeling came over me that there was going to be a message from Sarah."

"Does she sometimes send messages?"

"Never one in twenty years. But this feeling came over me and I had to go out and climb the cliff, though the wind nearly rolled me over it, and there was the *Santa Maria*."

"Do you often have that wish to go to the cliff and look for the *Santa Maria*?" Jim asked.

"I do, from time to time."

Until this moment, it seemed, the long memory of that old *Santa Maria* was so real to him that it still possessed him, even though we had denied that we knew anything of his story. Now we saw how moment by moment all the hope drained out of him and he suffered the agony of believing us. There were tears in his eyes as he said:

"Sure, you don't come from Sarah at all. You never heard of Sarah. The world is full of boats called *Santa Maria*. She's a new boat anyway, and a Connemara boat. Didn't I see that plain. The old *Santa Maria* was a Spanish boat. I'm just a foolish, simple old man with a head full of queer notions."

We were silent for a full minute. One of the kittens rolled over on its back, letting the warmth of the fire reach its pale-brown stomach. Then I said:

"Yes, our *Santa Maria* is a new boat. This is her first voyage."

Instantly he demanded:

"Why is she out on her first voyage with two boys only? A new boat always has the best sailors in the parish for her first voyage. Not disrespecting the two of you, of course."

"You can see what we did to her," I said bitterly. "After this, anyone that likes can disrespect us."

"What happened to you would happen to anyone—'twould even happen to Captain Hennessy, that sailed the Atlantic when I was a boy. There's no by-your-leave with a storm like that."

"Everyone in Rossmore said she was an unlucky boat," I said. "We should have heeded them."

"They were wrong, then," said the old man eagerly. "An unlucky boat would drown all that went on her. Aren't the two of you sitting here by the fire, without as much as a scratch on either of you? That's not an unlucky boat. Tell me now, why did they say those things about her?"

So we began at the beginning and told him the whole story of the building of the *Santa Maria*, of my grandfather's years of labor on her, of how she was finished by Maggie, and of how her father had entrusted her first voyage to me and had decided on her name, just before he died. We stretched the story out as long as we could, so as to divert his attention from his disappointment. At the end he said:

" 'Tis a strange history, and a strange name for a Rossmore boat to have. Maybe 'twas God sent you here, after all. Now I'll tell you my story. I'll redden up the fire a bit first, because a good fire is the half of life."

While he put more turf on the fire, I moved across and sat on the hob which was not occupied by the cats. I had an idea that his story would be a long one and I did not want to be prodded every half-minute with his bony knee, throughout the telling of it. Also, though he kept his house and all around it so neat and clean, his clothes were badly in the need of a washing. Perhaps he was afraid to wash them, I thought charitably, lest they might dissolve into shreds in the water, they were so worn. This was where Sarah, whoever she might be, could have made herself most useful. It astonished me to think how he had survived alone for so many years. In our house at home, when my mother went away for a day, everything seemed to go to ruin. Even the cats began to get ideas of freedom, so that she said it always took three or four days after she came back to get things under control.

When the old man had settled himself on his chair again, he began his story:

"This island is called Flaherty's Island. Maybe you heard of it by that name?"

Jim had heard of it once, he said. He knew that it was a long way from Rossmore, well out to sea from Carraroe where the nearest mainland was.

"It has a saint's name too, but it was called Flaherty's Island always because that was the name of everyone on it. I'm a Flaherty myself—Colman I was called, when there was anyone to call me by my name. I remember the time when there were fifteen families living on this island and seven or eight or ten children in every house. It was a cheerful place then. Everywhere you'd go, you'd see boys and girls minding geese, or sheep, or calves, going for water, doing a bit of milking. Sometimes when I go around by the road now I imagine I hear them running and playing and laughing, the way they used to do long ago.

"We had a school here then, and sometimes we had as many as seventy children in it. The teacher used to live in a little house beside the school—it's standing still. They did fine building in those days.

"It was a grand place to live. We used to have grand times when we'd be cutting turf, or threshing the bit of grain in the harvest, and at Christmas. Weddings were times for the best of fun. We'd be singing and dancing till the dawn of day. But sure, that's how it is over in Rossmore at the present time, isn't it?"

"It is," I said. "What happened to stop it here?"

"A lot of things. There were terrible famines, long before my time, as you know, and the people started going off to America where there was bread and work for all, as the song said, and the sun shone always. I don't know was that true, for I was never tempted to go there myself. One by one, the children went away, and we were mostly old people, and a few young ones that had got married here and were raising their own children. They weren't as poor then as their fathers had been because there was more land for every family. They had pigs and sheep and young cattle and horses. They'd go in to Galway on a fair day and they'd come home jingling with money.

"But they weren't contented. That's always the way. The

more people have, the less contented they are. Every letter from their brothers and sisters in America used to be tempting them away with the grand life they had over there. Plenty of money, they said. No work after six o'clock in the evening, they said. Your two hands loaded down with dollars every Friday or Saturday, they said. And the wide world before your children, that they could grow up to be millionaires with all the grand schools and colleges that were everywhere.

"That was what finished them, in the end. Every father saw his little boy driving a carriage and six. Every mother saw her daughter dressed out in silks and laces. One by one, the families set out for the New World—father, mother, and children—until there was no one left but myself and my family.

"Sarah was my youngest daughter. She wasn't my only child—oh, no. She had three brothers and two sisters. Eight we were in the house when they were all growing up together. We had plenty of good land and a bit of money in the bank in Galway, which seemed to me a mighty queer state of things for an islandman. My grandfather would break his sides laughing if he were to know that. They were good times, in a way, but every year the island got more and more lonesome as the young people grew up.

"Then my daughter Mary got married to an Inishownan man—only a couple of miles of sea between us. But the same year my wife died, God rest her soul. While she was here, she kept the house so lovely no one would ever think of leaving it. But afterwards it was different. It wasn't a year after we buried her over in Carraroe that my son Tom came in one evening and threw down the shovel and said: 'I'm off to America.'

"What could I say? He should have found a wife for himself that would content herself on our island. But I had to agree, and a few weeks later he was gone. We carried on for a couple of months and then Paddy said he'd be going too. He was a cheerful sort of boy, always laughing about something or other. He took his melodeon with him when he went and we never had a bit of music in the house afterwards. He wasn't gone three months till the girl that came after him was off, and then the last boy. One day, there was no one on the whole of Flaherty's Island but myself and Sarah. That all happened in one year."

"Didn't they ask you to go with them?" I asked, shocked at such callousness, as it seemed to me, in deserting the old man in this way.

"They did, sure. Many a time they asked me. But I was headstrong in those days, maybe the same as I am now. I said I wouldn't go. I said it was wrong to be flying out of the country when there wasn't a right reason for it. I said if God made you an Irishman, He meant you to be an Irishman. I said, how well the Aran people don't all leave their island and go careering off to America. They stay where they are, where they have a good way of living, and they're contented enough."

During this speech his voice had risen until by the end of it he was almost shouting. It was easy to imagine that the younger people had not emigrated without plenty of fierce and angry arguments.

"And I said I wouldn't go so far away from my wife's grave," the old man continued. "She was a Conneeley woman from Casla, that came out here to the island with me and I younger, and she never made a moan nor a complaint as long as I knew her, God rest her soul."

"Amen," we said, and Jim asked:

"What about Sarah? Didn't she want to go to America too?"

"Sarah said she would stay with me. She said I'd have to have someone to mind the house for me, to make the butter and feed the chickens. I thought she was a fine generous girl. She was a beauty, as I told you, and there was a MacDonagh man from Inishownan that had his eye on her. I'd have been contented enough if she had married him. They could have had this house and all the land, and he being an islandman born and bred would live happy enough here. She used to meet him when she'd go over to Inishownan to stay with her sister for the night, when I'd be gone in to the fair in Galway."

"Inishownan is near you?"

" 'Tis hardly a couple of miles."

"So you have a daughter there still? You go over to visit her sometimes, or she comes to visit you?" I asked, immensely relieved at the thought that the old man was not really as solitary as had first appeared.

"I never go there. She never comes here." Now I saw that his mouth had hardened into a tight, bitter line. His next words were forced out one by one, as if each were a torment to utter. "I hope I'll never lay an eye on her again, as long as there's life in me."

We did not know what to say to this. I began to wish myself a hundred miles from his comfortable fire. Not for the first time in my life, I reflected on the truth of the old saying that there is nothing wrong with the world, only with the people that are in it. In the name of contentment this old man seemed to have quarreled with his whole family. Jim had more courage than I had. He said after a moment's pause:

"I'd have thought you would be good friends with your daughter on Inishownan. She didn't go off to America like the rest of the family."

The old man gave a kind of hoot.

"Ho, no. She did not. She did worse. I had one left, one out of all my houseful of children, and she schemed and plotted till she got her away from me. There was a way for a daughter to treat her own father! The only comfort I had was that her mother was under the sod before it happened, that she didn't ever know the trickery and the roguery that went on."

"God look down on us!" I said, shocked through my whole being at such talk. "What did she do?"

"What didn't she do? I was an innocent, a fool, indeed. When I'd go in to Galway in the hooker I had, to a fair or a market, first I'd bring Sarah over to Inishownan, as I was saying, to stay a few days with Mary while I'd be away. Mary was older and I used to be thinking she could be advising Sarah, the way her mother would have done if she had been alive. I was hoping she'd make it up to marry the MacDonagh man. But her own sister, the last time I ever spoke to her, was evil enough to disrespect that man. He wasn't only after Sarah, she said. He was after the island too—the bit of land she'd have here. 'What is wrong with that?' I said. 'Doesn't it show he is a prudent, far-thinking kind of a man, that would make a good, providing husband and father?' And do you know what she said to me? 'Providing for himself, he is.' And why wouldn't he? Did she expect him to starve? Sure, every man has to think of providing. Doesn't the world know that?"

We hardly knew where to look. Fortunately he did not seem to expect an answer. He was brooding heavily to himself, twisting his wrinkled old hands in remembered fury at the difference in ideas that had existed between himself and Mary so long ago. It was easy for us to imagine how the older sister had wanted to save Sarah from marrying this fortune hunter. The island was a fine fortune for a girl to have. She would be lucky indeed if it were not coveted by a few greedy people. Of course we knew that the old man belonged to a generation that thought a girl would be immodest if she asked whom she was to marry. That was for her parents to arrange. The old man said in a tone full of quiet venom:

"What was Sarah doing over in Inishownan? Who was she talking to all evening long, with the blessing of her sister? A big Spanish sailorman, a foreigner from the north coast of Spain. He used to come in there in his little trawler——"

"The *Santa Maria*," I said.

"That was her name. Oh, he said he owned land as well, but how could you believe a foreigner without as much as a drop of Irish blood in him?"

He glared at each of us in turn, so that we felt quite guilty when we could make no answer.

"It wasn't Sarah's fault," he went on, "though she was led away in the end to wrong her father. If she had asked me, I would have said no, that she could not marry a man that wasn't of her own race and kind. But she never asked me. She never told me about him at all." His voice went so low now that he almost seemed to be talking to himself. "I went to Galway in August, just twenty years ago. I had big lambs to sell, I remember well, and I got a good price for them. I bought a piece of cloth for Sarah to make a dress with, blue cloth with little white flowers on it. It's there in the press still. I came home on my own, all the way out from Galway. I had a Carraroe man with me to help me with the lambs, but I left him behind in Galway because he had some business of his own to do. It was a beautiful day, and with a grand wind, and I was delighted with myself all the way home and I thinking of the welcome I'd get from Sarah.

"I called in at Inishownan to fetch her. Mary said she was gone over already, in the Spaniard's boat. I didn't take much notice of that. I thought maybe she wanted to have the fire going and the bread baked before I'd come. And there were cows to milk as well—you can never leave a cow for more than a few hours. We used to leave a calf in with them when we'd be away, to do a bit of milking for us.

"I was thinking what a fine girl Sarah was, and I was sailing in to the quay. She wasn't there to meet me. Above at the house she'd be, of course. And the Spaniard must be gone, because there wasn't a trace of his boat to be seen.

"Up with me, to the house. I wasn't far off it when I heard the cows bellowing, the way they do be complaining when they're not milked. I couldn't make that out at all—why she wouldn't run to milk them first after being away so long.

"When I got to the house I saw that the cows were all around it, as you might say calling to her to come out. I got a fright on me when I saw that. I ran up to the house. She wasn't there, nor a soul other. I started looking around the sheds outside, thinking she might have fallen and hurt herself. I didn't know what to think. Not a sign of her anywhere. I went farther away, to the fields and up the hill, and at last I climbed the cliff for a view of that part of the island.

"Then I saw the *Santa Maria*. She was anchored off the shore, right where your *Santa Maria* is now. It was a lovely evening. The wind had dropped at sunset, the way it often does. There was a dinghy and two people in it, halfway between the trawler and the shore. First I thought they were coming ashore and I let a big shout out of me to show that I was there. I had never met that Spanish sailorman, though I knew about him from hearing the Inishownan people talking. But not a one of them had told me rightly what kind of a person he was.

"When they heard the shout, Sarah and the Spaniard looked up at the cliff at once. Then I saw that it was heading for the trawler they were. After one second, the man got the oars going again and he rowing as if the devil was after him. I didn't know what to make of that. There was Sarah, waving to me. When they got alongside, they climbed aboard by a rope ladder. Then they hauled up the dinghy by ropes, and the next thing they got up steam and began to sail away. There was I watching them like a fool. They were under weigh before I began to guess what was happening. I watched them until it was too dark to see them any more.

"I got a foolish idea into my head that they would turn around after a while and come back. That made me stay there half the night, kneeling on the grass that was as cold as a grave in the darkness and listening to those queer birds that only come out in the nighttime to torment people with their lonesome whistling.

"The moon was gone down, I remember well, when the night changed. It happened little by little, so that at first I hardly knew it was no longer a fine August night. I felt the wind nipping me, and I thought it was the lateness of the hour. Then I noticed that the sea was growling below on the rocks. The wind got a bit stronger, and I thought in the back of my mind that it would be a good day tomorrow for the men that were still in Galway after the fair, and that would be sailing home to their own places on the coast and in the islands.

"Even when there was half a gale blowing, I still knelt there like a bullock that would be after falling down and that won't make any shift to get himself up again. I knew she was gone away with the Spaniard and that was all I could hold in my head. But when the wind was so strong that it nearly sent me over the cliff, I came to my senses.

"I never stood up. I remember that. I crawled down off the cliff on my hands and knees, and that's how I came to the sheltered place. God of power, that was a night! 'Twas for all the world like the storm we had today, as I told you. The rain fell the way it did in the time of Noah. The wind roared and shouted till you'd think you'd lose your hearing. Long before the night was over, I was sure that Sarah and the Spaniard and any other crew of the trawler must surely be dead and drowned. I swore then that if she came back, I wouldn't say a single word against her, only thank God she was alive.

"I thought for a long time that she must have died in that storm. I went every day for months afterwards to see would her body come sailing in to me, or a piece of the boat, or any sign of what happened to it. They found the body of a Spanish sailor off Lettermore a couple of weeks later, but the people there knew him and they said he came from another boat."

"And did you never hear if she came safely to Spain?"

"Oh, yes. She came safely."

"And you know she's still alive?"

"I have heard that she is."

"Does she write letters, perhaps, to you or to her sister?"

"She never wrote a letter to me but once. Maybe she writes to her sister. If she does, I don't want to hear of it. I sent a message to her sister to say that I hope I'll never lay living eyes on her again, but that I'll come after I'm dead. That's when I'll come to her!"

"God bless us! That's a terrible sin!" said Jim before he could stop himself.

"There's sins and sins," said the old fellow. "What about her sin against me?"

"You should leave that to God," Jim said.

"God helps them that help themselves, I always heard," said he. "Oh, yes, I sent Mary that message. The priest over in Inishownan got to hear of it. She went howling to him, I suppose. Anyway he came over here one fine day, with two Inishownan men rowing the currach, and he told me 'twas un-Christian to be threatening, that I should forgive all wrongs. I'll forgive it when I meet her in the next world, I told him, and not a minute before."

We were dumbfounded at this ferocity. After a long pause I asked:

"And did the priest go away satisfied?"

"He did not, nor satisfied. He argued and argued, but I couldn't get the picture of Sarah out of my mind and I wouldn't agree with him. He wanted me to go over to Inishownan and make friends with Mary again. It takes two to be friends, I said to him, and she's no friend of mine."

"And did he never come again?"

"Oh, yes. He comes often. Like myself, he's getting old,

but he doesn't forget to come. He's the only visitor I have from Inishownan now. He brings me news of my grand-children—fine strong men he says they are, and a credit to me, though they have the bad drop in them from their mother."

We thought it better not to answer this. I asked:

"What about the ones that went to America?"

"They write letters and I write letters, but they don't ever come home. They know the way it is between me and Mary, for I told them. The last time the priest was here, he had a different tune. I should go over to Inishownan and live with Mary in my old age, he said—the way she could look after me. Even if I had a mind to, I wouldn't do it. I'm staying here in my own house, I told him, until Sarah comes back. As sure as you're sitting there, some day she will come back."

"That's why you were down at the cliff today, waiting for Sarah?"

"Yes. I nearly lost my mind when I saw the *Santa Maria* below on the rocks."

By this time it was pitch dark outside. The wind still thundered in the chimney, occasionally lifting a little twirl of soft brown ash with a down draught. We both felt desperately tired, though we could see by the old wall clock that it was only half-past ten. Colman Flaherty got up and went to the pile of turf.

"We'll make a little pot of *brochán* when the fire is red again," he said. "Do you like *brochán*? It's what I always have before going to bed."

We told him that it would satisfy us very well. It is a thin porridge made with milk and loaded with sugar, and it has a powerful effect of sending one to sleep. He made it expertly, as he did everything, and presently he was filling a mug for each of us. He turned his back to us while he put a jet of poiteen into his own mug, and then he said apologetically as he handed us ours:

"Old people do need a little drop of the hard stuff from

time to time. Thinking about Sarah made me terrib e cross
this evening."

We assured him that we had no mind for poiteen in our
brochán.

"Good boys," he said. "Good boys. 'Tis fine stuff without any poiteen."

"Sarah wrote you one letter?" I said after a pause.

"Yes."

"And did you write to her?"

"I wrote one letter to her. I told her that I'd wait here for her until the crack of doom. I told her she could come any time, even if I was dead, for my soul would be here in this house, waiting for her."

"God help us!" said Jim. "You threatened to haunt her too?"

Fortunately the old man did not notice that we were both amused rather than terrified at this idea. He took a long, windy swallow of his *brochán.*

"And how could I lie easy?" he demanded. "Tell me that! How could I lie in peace in my grave and my own flesh and blood risen up against me? Sarah's letter came from a village in Spain called Commillas. Full of flowers, she said, and right on the blue sea. She said the coast in those parts is like Ireland—little green hills and stone walls—so that she didn't feel lonesome at all. She said the trawlers go from there to Ireland for the fishing and that when the men came back they brought her all the news. She said she had a fine house of her own with everything in it that a woman could want."

"That was a very good letter," I said. "Did she say anything in it about coming back?"

"Not a word. That's why I wrote to her the way I did. She said too that her husband was a fine man, well thought of by everyone, and that he owned a farm of land as well as his trawler. Oh, she made up a good case for him, and no mistake."

"Maybe it was all true," I said.

He gave a little snarling laugh.

"How could it be true? A man that would steal my daughter from under my nose—how could you have any trust in a man like that?"

We did not dare to defend the absent Spaniard any further. Obviously the old man had hated him for so long that he could not bear to think he might have some virtues. One thing seemed clear enough, however, and that was that he did not hate Sarah. Though he had said that his ghost would wait for her until she came, his tone had not had the venomous ring to it that we had heard when he spoke of haunting his daughter Mary. Looking across at him from the hob, I thought what an unsavory ghost he would make, with his rags and his wild hair and his glowing, angry eyes.

As soon as we had finished the *brochán*, the old man stood up.

"You can both sleep in Sarah's room," he said. "It's a fine, dry room, there behind the fireplace." He cocked his head to listen to the wind. "The storm is easing off. The whistle is gone out of it. Tomorrow we'll go down and see what we can do for the *Santa Maria*."

"If she's still there."

"She'll be there, all right," he said. "She has to be there, with the wind from the west. She's as safe as if she were inside in the docks in Galway."

He seemed so sure of this that we allowed ourselves to be comforted. A moment later, he left us alone in Sarah's room. It was a lovely room. The candlelight shone on white curtains embroidered with flying birds. There was a huge bed with a white quilt. In the dim light we could just see that both the quilt and the curtains were really a pale gray, from the need of washing. Still, to us the room looked then like a little palace.

"The bed is dry, sure enough," Jim said softly, "but if it were a bog, I'd sleep in it tonight."

(4)

It was broad daylight when we awoke. One would think
that there had never been a storm. Through the thin curtains
the sun shone strongly and the patch of light that we could
see as we lay in bed was a luminous blue. The air seemed to
be full of the twittering of birds. The hens were out and we
could hear their peaceful clucking and then the sound of the
old man's voice calling to them:

"Chookie-chookie! Choo-ookie-chookie!"

His voice was cracked and high, rather like the voice of a
hen, indeed, or perhaps like an old woman's. He crossed the
window, darkening it for a moment, scattering food from a
dish.

On his way back, he rapped sharply on the glass and called
out:

"Up, lazybones! Could ye sleep all day?"

When we reached the kitchen, we found that he had been
making bread. Its sweet, steamy smell filled the room. He
cut hot slices from the new loaf and gave them to us with
goat's milk, for breakfast. While we ate, he hurried in and
out with feed for his pigs and his ducks.

"I should rear a few calves again," he said. "Maybe I will,
someday. When you have cows all your life, it's a queer thing
to be depending on goats. My pigs do well. I buy them small

and rear them up. They get their health good, here. Everyone gets their health on this island."

He certainly was healthy enough himself. He sprang
around, doing the household tasks, as lively as a boy. When
we had finished, he said:

"Now we can go down and look at the boat. We're in luck,
with such a good day. Sometimes the sea would be rough for
a week after a storm like that. It's like glass today."

It was indeed as smooth a sea as I had ever seen in my life.
To look at it now, one would never believe that it could have
reared itself up into horrifying mountains and cliffs that had
threatened our very lives yesterday. I almost wept at the
thought that if we were under that quiet sea now, it would
lie as heavy on us as if it had been a mass of thundering
waves.

"How can we send word to our parents that we are safe?"
I asked the old man as we walked to the beach where the
Santa Maria was. "We must tell them as soon as possible that
we are alive."

"I could take you over to Carraroe in my own boat," he
said. "From there you could be home in a couple of hours."

"We don't want to go home," I said. "We only want to
send word. After last night, they'll be holding a wake for each
of us today. They won't believe anyone could ever live
through a storm like that."

"They won't believe it, indeed," Colman said. "But Sarah
lived through as bad, long ago."

"They won't have heard of that," I said impatiently.

"And why don't you want to go home at once?" he asked,
stopping in front of us on the path and turning around to
look us over.

We had to stop too, and we had to give a straight answer
to that question. I knew why I didn't want to go back. I
guessed that Jim knew too, but he left all the explanation to
me.

54

"We don't want to go back," I said, "because if we do it will be as if we are condemning the *Santa Maria.* For more than ten years, while she was building, she stood outside my grandfather's door. Some of the men could come for her now, I suppose, and patch her up and take her home. But if they do, I can tell you for certain sure that neither they nor anyone else will ever sail in her again. She'll stand outside my grandfather's door until her bones are white. Every time that Maggie goes out of the house, there will be the boat to shame her."

"But you weren't drowned from the *Santa Maria,*" Colman said. "It's only when someone is drowned from a boat that she is abandoned like that."

"I'm thinking they'll make an exception for the *Santa Maria,*" said Jim. "She was supposed to be such a wonder, they'll say, and she couldn't keep off the rocks on her first day out. They won't say a word against her except that, maybe, but it will happen somehow that no one will want to risk taking her out again."

"So it would be better for us to take her for another cruise, where she won't come to any harm, and bring her home safe," I said.

"Supposing you take her for that other cruise and she doesn't come home safe?"

"She'll come safe."

"You have faith in your boat," said Colman.

We could see that he himself was inclined to believe that the *Santa Maria* might be unlucky, though it was he who had pointed out that a bad boat is one that drowns her passengers. I trusted that boat. I remembered how she had seemed almost to fly along the sea when it was doing its best to swallow her up and crunch her bones. An idea came to me which was too foolish to express: that if Flaherty's Island had not got in her way, she would have weathered that storm perfectly. I knew there was truth in this notion. Even a good boat can't keep off a lee shore forever. If the wind had been a few points more to the north, we would have been blown away out into the Atlantic, none the worse except for the long drag home.

Colman said:

" 'Tis true for you that this trip won't have improved the boat's reputation. Supposing we repair her ourselves and let you sail her home: is that what you're thinking of?"

"That would be only a short cruise," I said. "It wouldn't take a great boat to sail from here to Rossmore on a good day."

"God help us, what are you thinking of? Are you planning to sail the Atlantic Ocean, like Saint Brendan, or Captain Hennessy? Neither of them had a bigger boat than your *Santa Maria*."

From where we stood, high on the cliff, we could see her lying on the beach below us. She looked very small and helpless there.

"I wasn't thinking of sailing the Atlantic," I said. "I was thinking of sailing to Commillas."

He went as still as a stone. Then he gave a little skip on the path and a high, whinnying laugh.

"To Commillas! Of course that is where the *Santa Maria* should go. And when ye come back, ye'll be the talk of the world forever after, like Mael Dúin or any of the other old heroes they do tell about in the stories. When you come back——" He stopped and looked from one of us to the other. "Ye'll surely come back."

"She's a good boat," Jim said. "She'd sail to the islands of Greece, as well as Mael Dúin's boat did."

"And you'll bring Sarah back with you?"

"If she'll come."

Such a look of longing came into his face at this that we knew there could be no question of changing our minds now. It was an enormous undertaking. Until the moment when I had expressed it, I had hardly known clearly that this was what we must do. Obviously Jim had not thought of it at all. He looked excited and terrified at the prospect, and I could see by the impatient looks he kept turning on me that he was burning to discuss the whole project with me alone. To the old man it must have seemed as if we had talked half the night about the plan. As we continued on our way down to the shore, he kept turning and stopping to ask us for details of our experience as sailors in order, of course, to estimate our chances of getting to Commillas and back alive.

"Ye went into Galway? Ye went to Aran? Now that can be a tricky business. You're nearly safer out in the wide ocean than you would be in the neighborhood of the cliffs of Moher and the islands. There's queer old currents there that you don't meet at all on the wide ocean."

We did not tell him that we had never sailed to these distant places alone.

"I can see why ye don't want to go home, all right," Colman said when we reached the beach. He chuckled like a hen. "I can imagine how the news would be received at home, that ye were planning a cruise to Spain, when ye couldn't get around Galway Bay without running aground." He shook his head in appreciation of our parents' fury at not being consulted beforehand. "Ye'll get a queer welcome when ye come back. Ye will come back?" he finished anxiously.

"Of course we'll come back."

"Don't be cross, a-mac," he said, squeezing my arm with a skinny claw. "I won't ask it again. 'Tis only that I'm anxious about Sarah."

This morning, the shore was bathed in the heat of the sun. Not a breath of wind moved. Tiny waves crackled on the sea's edge where the small pebbles and shells were. Between the black rocks, the sea lay smooth and calm, lined with gentle ripples and reflecting a clear blue sky. The tide was low, and our poor *Santa Maria* lay on her side, beached, and looking very much as I had imagined she would be when she would lie abandoned outside Maggie's door. Colman Flaherty went crawling over to her, seeming not to feel the sharp rocks under his horny feet while he examined every inch of her timbers.

"She's not bad, not bad at all. There's hardly a day's work in repairing her. We'll have to patch her up quick to keep the tide out, and then we'll float her in another piece. We'll patch her with canvas. I have lots of it at home, that I use for mending my currach. Maybe ye have a bit of canvas on board?"

"Not an inch but the sails. We didn't expect to need it."

"I'll go up and get mine, then. Let the two of ye stay here and keep an eye on her. The tide won't be up to her for a while yet."

He set off at a run up the beach, and we could see him a minute later clambering up the cliff path without slowing down—like a goat. We watched him until he had reached the top and then we turned back to the *Santa Maria.*

"We were lucky that she struck at high tide," Jim said. "If it had been low tide, when the sea would come up over her, she'd have been washed away and we'd never see her again."

"I've just been wondering what kind of a welcome we'll get from Sarah when we get to Commillas," I said.

Jim gave a short laugh.

"You should have thought of that before you offered to go," he said. "I've been wondering about that too."

"She can't eat us," I said uneasily. Then I said, after a moment's pause: "If you don't want to go, we can still back out of it."

"Which of us is going to tell the old fellow that we have changed our minds?"

"I haven't changed my mind."

"Neither have I. But there's another thing: do you think he may want to come with us?"

"He's too old."

Even as I said this, it occurred to me that it might be a fine thing if we could persuade him to come. He was evidently a good sailor, as he would have to be, living on this remote island. He had spoken of sailing out from Galway alone, which is not easy. He could look after all the navigation so that we would not finish in the Canary Islands. A third member of the party would mean that when one of us slept the other would not be alone. He was a good cook, and he was so neat around the house that one could tell he would be handy on a boat. There were many advantages, and yet I found myself hoping that he would not want to come with us.

"What would we do if he were to become ill on the way?" I said. "What would we do if he were to die? Or if Sarah refused to see him when he arrived? Or if he has no other clothes to wear and would walk up through her village in those rags, telling everyone that he is her father?"

"Maybe he has some decent clothes at home. We'll find out later, about that."

Since we had decided to go to Spain, the whole world had changed. So many difficulties crowded in on us that it would be days before we would have sorted them out. We knew that the voyage was possible, and that was all. How dangerous it would be we did not know. We wanted to take the *Santa Maria* on a long cruise, to feel again the power stored up in her, and it seemed fitting that such a noble little ship should have such a fine purpose as to make peace between Sarah and her father at last.

Within a quarter of an hour, the old man came hopping and climbing down the cliff path again. He had a bundle of tools rolled up in a piece of strong canvas of the kind used for building currachs, and a little can of hot tar with a brush sticking out of it.

"I heated up the tar while I was searching out the canvas," he said. "I always keep a little can of it handy for when I'll need it."

Then he began to call out questions: had we cleaned the seaweed out of the boat? Had we bailed out the water that was lodged in her? We had not thought of these things, of course. With one eye on the advancing tide, he set to work at nailing a double patch of canvas over the foot-square hole. When he had finished, the tar was still soft enough to be painted over the canvas.

In the meantime, we had been cleaning out the inside of the boat. The incoming tide was washing around our feet when this was finished. Colman took a mooring rope over the bows and made it fast to a rock higher up the shore.

"We could have moored her where she was," he said, "but the closer in she is, the more time we'll have to work on her."

It was a great moment for us when we saw her floating free again. She had a list on her good side, because Colman had made us move her ballast of stones over there to make sure that she would rest with her damaged side up when the tide would go down again. As the tide rose, he hauled her closer in, until he judged that she would come no nearer without grounding. Then he shortened the mooring rope and said:

"We'll wait a while now, till she settles. The tide is on the turn."

That half hour of waiting was as long as the whole morning. Very slowly the tide began to recede, leaving the wet rocks glistening in the hot sunshine. Slowly the orange-colored weed appeared, first floating on the surface and then gradually lying slackly against the rocks. A few sea gulls came to the edge of the sea, as they always do after high tide, dropping with a plop like a stone into the water when they spotted a fish. Little by little the *Santa Maria* settled on the rocks, gently and slowly. Then Colman said:

"I had a look for some timber when I went up for the

canvas, and I don't like the few bits that are there. I'll bring some back from Carraroe when I go there in the afternoon. And I'll send your message at the same time."

"If you send a telegram, they'll be over from Rossmore for us in a couple of hours. They'll see on it that it came from Carraroe——"

He looked at me pityingly and said:

"I didn't come down in the last shower. I have better ways of sending messages than by telegram—ways that were invented long before the telegraph, too."

For some reason, it would have seemed uncivil to have asked him what these ways were. He made me describe exactly where we lived and give him our fathers' first names, so that there would be no doubt that the message would reach the right people, so he said.

When we got back to the house, he sent us to see if there were any eggs in the hen house. We found six.

"Two each," he said. "You see, my hens can count. And there will be six more in the evening, from the ones that are laying out. They think I won't find where they're hiding their eggs, but I have them spotted, all right. And we'll have a fine piece of bacon in the evening. Are ye any good to cook bacon?"

I said that I had often seen my mother do it and that we would be able to follow his instructions. He climbed onto the kitchen table and hacked a piece of bacon six inches thick from the long side that hung from the rafters.

"That's the stuff," he said admiringly, turning it over and over in his hands. "Into the pot with it at six o'clock. At seven you'll throw a head of cabbage in after it, and mind you wash it well first. I only want one kind of meat with my dinner. You can put a pot of potatoes to boil on the hearth. I'll be home at half-past seven and the dinner will be ready. There's no king eats the way I do," he finished proudly.

"I can believe that," I said solemnly.

We had the eggs boiled and some more of his soda-bread, washed down with strong-tasting goat's milk. Colman smacked his lips over the milk.

"A great thing about goat's milk is that it never tastes the same two days running. A goat ranges everywhere she fancies and she eats a bite of everything. Then she passes all those tastes on to the milk."

It was only when he had said this that I realized that I had drunk a whole mugful of that interesting milk, which I would never have touched at home.

When we had finished eating, Colman made us go outside while he got out the money that he would need to buy the timber, and some groceries he said he needed from Carraroe.

"It's not that I don't trust ye," he said, "but what ye don't know won't trouble ye. I don't know why I hide my money at all, because no one ever comes to this island except the priest once a month."

As we walked down to the place where he kept his currach, he instructed us about minding the fire and milking the goats if they came around asking for it, and he renewed all his instructions about cooking the dinner. We were hardly listening to him, because we were so much interested in seeing the rest of the island. Until now, we had only seen the part between the house and the cliff. Now we found that the land sloped downwards toward a long sandy beach, which faced across to the Connemara shore. This seemed to be about five miles away, judging by the bluish haze that hung over the mountains there. On such a clear day, we could easily see a cluster of white houses on the mainland. Colman said:

"That's Carraroe, over there. Sometimes I don't see it for a month."

"It's a long way to go in a currach," I said.

"The men we reared when I was young wouldn't call that a long way," he said. "There's times of the year when I don't try to get there, for the reason that I know I wouldn't succeed. But on a day like today it's no bother at all—I'll be over in an hour and a half, easy."

He had a hooker too, which he kept in a little natural harbor formed of two long fingers of rock at one end of the beach. He brought us to look at it before he set out in the currach. It was a small hooker, more like what we call a gleoiteog, but he said that it was big enough for his needs and that he had often brought sheep in it to Galway. For bringing cattle or horses he used to call on his neighbors from Inishownan, in the days when he was on speaking terms with them, before his daughter ran off with the Spaniard. Since then he had never set foot on Inishownan. We noticed that he did not lift his eyes to look at the neighboring island, which showed greenly a couple of miles away from where his boat was moored.

We helped him carry the currach down to the edge of the sea, from the top of the beach. In a moment he had skipped aboard and was floating a yard off the shore.

"God speed you!" we called out to him.

He worked the oars like a man in a frenzy, and within a few minutes he and his boat had become a little black speck.

We felt suddenly lonely and abandoned. The island seemed to have become a more desolate place than ever. We went at once to look again at Colman's hooker, as if to prove to ourselves that we were not really prisoners. Then we set out to explore the rest of the island.

It was a strange experience. Everywhere there were little ruined houses in varying stages of decay. One could tell which ones had been abandoned earliest by the growth of ivy on the walls. Grass-grown lanes led up to empty doorways. Badgers and foxes had taken possession of many of the houses, and there were jackdaws' nests in the chimneys. We found the school, with the teacher's house close by. A stone plaque gave the date of its building, 1851. Of all the ruins, the school and the teacher's house were the only ones that

were partly roofed. This was because they had once been slated. All the other houses had been thatched, and the thatch and the rotted rafters had long since collapsed inside.

Slowly we walked back by the wandering lanes until we came in sight of Colman's house. It warmed our hearts to see it, like finding a healthy man on an island where everyone has died of plague.

Still it seemed too fine and clear a day to be spent inside. We passed by the house on its left-hand side and climbed the little hill behind it. There we lay down on the sloping grass, which was soft and clean, and rested our heads on our hands. From here we could see downhill a little way, to where a shoulder of land cut off the view of the sea. It was very quiet.

At this time of the afternoon, even the sea gulls were resting
from their usual squalling arguments. Only the goats were
moving. There seemed to be at least half a dozen of them.
As we lay there, they came around the side of the hill, not all
together, but keeping their independence from each other as
goats usually do. They cropped the grass and then lifted
their heads to stare with their queer yellow eyes that had
something unpleasantly human in them.

While we watched, all the goats moved up the hill together, crowding into a single group, prancing and jumping
in their hurry. The billy goat stayed behind them, almost as
if he were herding them along. We watched without a word,
aware that something had startled them. Then, around the
shoulder of the hill, came the figure of a man. He walked
slowly, gazing straight ahead of him toward the house. We
lay as still as if we were dead. The man moved on and came
into the lane that led to the house. With the same slow,
measured step, he went right up to the window of the kitchen
and paused while he peered inside. From that window he
moved to the window of Sarah's room. I felt ridiculously glad
that we had tidied everything up before going out in the
morning.

A moment later he had opened the door and had slipped
inside.

Until then, I had been sure that he was a ghost. The deso-
lation of the island had affected me, I suppose, and I knew
well that an island where there were so many ruins must
surely have at least one ghost. But when we saw that he had
to open the door to go into the house, we both sat up straight.

"He's a thief, that fellow," said Jim in a low voice.
"There's two of us."

We said no more but hurled ourselves down the hill. We
rushed into the kitchen, nearly falling over each other's heels,
expecting to find him ransacking the chest or the dresser.
Instead, he was standing quite still in the middle of the room,
looking around him like a man in a dream.

He was a middle-aged man, perhaps the age of my father,
very thin and spare. His narrowed eyes and his tight mouth
gave him a look of ferocity, so that we dropped back in alarm.
He seized that moment of our doubt. As quick as a shadow,
he fled out of the house and down the hill toward the beach.
After a moment of shock at the suddenness of this, we ran

outside and followed him a piece of the way, until we had a good view of the long strand.

A currach was drawn up at one end of it. Within a few minutes, he had reached it and was putting out to sea. Then with a few strokes of the oars, he rounded the long spur of rocks which formed one side of Colman's harbor and disappeared from our view.

We felt as exhausted as if we had had to do battle with him, so that we could only stand there gazing at the point where we had last seen him, as if we expected him to reappear. At last I said:

"He won't come back."

"I thought he was a ghost," Jim said, "he moved so quietly and slowly. He was in no hurry, that's certain."

"He must have seen Colman going off," I said. "Perhaps he was just curious. If he had nothing else to do, he might have wanted to see how things were going on this island."

"Perhaps. Yes, that could be. And still I have an idea that he wasn't coming for the first time. If you ask me, I'd say he comes very often."

"Colman said that no one comes except the priest."

"Colman is an innocent. If that man comes often, he waits until Colman has gone to Carraroe."

"What will we say to Colman when he comes back? Will we tell him what we saw?"

We could not decide what to do about it. Our first idea, of course, was to tell Colman the moment he put his foot ashore that he had had a visitor who seemed to know his way about the island very well indeed. Then we began to wonder whether this would be cruel. Colman was obliged to go to Carraroe sometimes. If he did not know that his island was visited in his absence, would it not be better to leave him in peace? He could do little or nothing to protect his property, except perhaps to lock the front door when he went away for a day. It seemed to us a kind of sin to destroy the remains of his trust in his neighbors.

We argued about it all the time while we made up the fire and hung the pot of water on the crane to boil. We went outside for a head of cabbage from the garden beside the house, and remembering Colman's instructions we washed it carefully in the stream that ran out of the well. Over all the island the air was still and warm. We could hear busy insects ticking in the grass, and an occasional birdcall, and that queer, sniggering sound that goats make. Colman's pigs were all asleep, having flopped down in the cool mud where water was lodged at one end of their little field. Even the hens were silent, asleep in the dusty place that they had scratched up close to the house. One would think that in all the world there was no happier place than this island, that there could never be dissension, or suspicion, or spying here—nothing but brotherly love and charity.

"How does he put down his days, alone in this place?" Jim asked suddenly. "Wouldn't you think he'd be over to see his daughter, if it was only for a bit of company?"

"It wouldn't suit me," I said, "but he was bred to it and that's why he's able to put up with it."

Over in Rossmore, everyone pitied the islanders. They were often richer than we were, and their land was free of many of the diseases that afflicted ours. Still the Connemara people felt that it was a terrible thing to have no road out of your land, leading to a town, and to have to take to the sea when you had business to do with the outside world.

A strange thing I had noticed, however, was that the island people felt equally sorry for us. They despised our boggy land and said that we lived on fish, like seals. *Bádóiri*, they called us—boatmen—and they could put a world of insult into that innocent-sounding word. This did not mean that there were not many friendships between island people and the mainlanders, but neither side could imagine himself living as the other did.

We put the piece of bacon in the pot, and an hour later we sent the cabbage in after it. Then we took some red sods of turf out of the fire and broke them with the tongs, and put a little three-legged pot full of potatoes to boil on them. We got our mugs for milk, and horn-handled knives and forks to eat with. All of this kept us busy, but I wished for once that the evening were not still as bright as day. It would have been a comfort to us to have been able to light the lamp and shut the door.

Jim gave a little shriek when a nanny goat poked her head in at the door and said softly:

"Meh-heh-heh-heh!"

He recovered himself in a moment.

"I know what you want," he said. "Where are the rest of ye?"

As if they had understood him, five more goat voices answered from outside.

There were two big shining cans waiting on a bench by the back door. We took one each, and settled down to milk the six goats. We were still occupied with this when Colman came up the lane with his sack of groceries on his shoulder. He stopped to look at us with delight.

"Two fine men I have to work for me," he said admiringly. "If ye would stay with me, I'd never have to do a hand's turn again."

(5)

Over supper, Colman told us how he had fared in Carraroe. We soon discovered that he was one of those people who feel the need to tell you every single detail of what they have done. Nothing whatever was left to our imagination. It seemed to us, at least, that he described every wave that he crossed on his way, and he certainly did describe fish and seals and lobster pots and fishing nets and other boats, that had taken his attention. Once or twice we tried to hurry him up but he would not.

"Haven't we all night?" he said. "Where's the hurry? There's a right and a wrong way to tell a story."

Little by little we found out what had happened. He had reached Carraroe in good time and had gone at once to Mac-Donagh's shop. He always went there, he said, because you could get everything that any reasonable person could possibly want in it: nets and tools and timber and nails and paint and groceries of all kinds, as well as beds and mattresses and blankets, though these were not the kind of thing he usually needed.

Mrs. MacDonagh knew him well and she invited him into the kitchen.

"She was cooking the dinner, and what do you think she had down in the pot but a fine piece of bacon and a head of

white cabbage. And she had another pot with enough potatoes in it to feed a regiment. She put me sitting at the table
and I was there chatting to her until the dinner was ready.
Oh, a fine, neighborly woman, that you wouldn't meet the
like of in the whole of west Connacht."

"Had she heard of the *Santa Maria?*" I could not restrain
myself from asking.

"I'm coming to that in a moment," said the old fellow
maddeningly. "I wasn't going to ask it straight out, of course,
the way I'm thinking you would do. If I did that, she might
say to herself: 'Now, how could he have heard of that boat
unless itself or a piece of it, or one of its passengers, God help
us, was washed up on Flaherty's Island by the tide? He didn't
hear it from the seals, nor from the mackerel either.' Oh,
she's a clever woman, Mrs. MacDonagh, and a handsome
woman too, though she's not as young as she might be.

"I didn't say a word about boats or shipping until we all
started on the dinner. There was Mrs. MacDonagh and Tom,
her husband, and their two sons John and James, and their
daughter Kate—the one that didn't go to America."

I caught Jim's eye at this but we managed to make no sign.
Colman went on:

" 'Twas a grand dinner and we made a good start on it before I said, careless like: 'Any new thing to tell?' It's no use
to look too curious, if you want people to tell you the news.
If you look as if you don't care a tinker's dam for their news,
they'll be wanting to shake you up. They'll be dredging their
brains for some story to bring a surprised look on you. So I
just said, nice and careless: 'Have you any new story?' In one
second, there was Mrs. MacDonagh telling me everything I
wanted to know and more besides, and her husband Tom
adding in pieces that she left out. There was a hooker lost
hereabouts yesterday, she said, a brand-new hooker that had
never been out of the quay of Rossmore before, and two fine
boys in it. She said it was a queer boat with a queer story

71

behind it, and that it couldn't have luck. She said the old man that built it was daft, and the daughter that finished it after he was dead was no better. She said there's wailing and lamenting over in Rossmore that would draw a tear from a stone."

This was exactly what we had feared. I said sharply:

"And what did you say to that? Did you say we are safe and sound? Did you send a message to Rossmore?"

"Of course I sent a message," he said indignantly, "but I didn't say to the MacDonaghs there and then that you're safe and sound. That would have been as good as inviting the lifeboat out to take ye away, and then I'd never see Sarah again in this life."

I had forgotten about Sarah for the moment.

"So you sent a message," I said.

"Of course. By this time they all know in Rossmore that ye're still in the land of the living. I had to stay a long time in MacDonagh's, to hear the rest of the story about the *Santa Maria* and the two fine boys that were lost with her. You should hear the way they talked about the two of you! It seems that no finer boys ever stood up than yourselves, the pride of your fathers and mothers, the hope of Rossmore. I wouldn't mind having a reputation like that myself."

We were very much surprised at this. All our lives we had been given to understand that if we were not extremely lucky we should end our lives in jail, if not on the gallows. Every injury done to property, everything lost or mislaid was blamed on us and on the other boys in the neighborhood, so that it would have seemed that we went from house to house all day doing little bits of damage. If the hens didn't lay, we had stolen the eggs. If the rope or the shears couldn't be found, we had removed them for illegal games. If the water bucket was empty, we had wasted it. So it went on, and our mothers made it plain that they were fighting with all their strength to save us from the fate to which we were rushing headlong.

It was sweet news, then, to hear that we were respected at least when we were thought to be dead.

"We sat a good while over dinner," Colman went on. "It was past five o'clock when we got up from the table. They eat their dinner late, which was well for me. I'd have got nothing if they had it at a decent time. Well, then I went into the shop and I ordered my timber and the other stuff—tea and butter and sugar, and a bit of flour. Then I went off outside to take the air while they would be getting the things ready, and after a while I took a little small walk up as far as Sabina Flaherty's. That's my own second cousin, she being a first cousin of my father, though she's the one age with me."

I was curious for a moment about this relationship, but I dared not ask a question lest Colman might embark on a long account of his family history. He looked ready for that. It was something in the stretch of his legs that warned me.

"I didn't go to Sabina's for dinner," he went on. "I said to myself that a bird in the hand is worth two in the bush, and that maybe when I'd get to Sabina's the dinner would be over, or maybe they wouldn't be having a fine piece of bacon the way they were in MacDonagh's. This time of the year, they do be all slaughtering the old hens and they're stringy, not disrespecting them. Oh, yes, I knew I had my own bacon and cabbage at home, and two fine cooks to ready it for me, but I thought to myself 'twould be like denying God's goodness not to have the second dinner when it was there under my nose."

"Did Sabina send the message for you?"

"She did not, then, for Sabina couldn't be trusted with a story like that. She's a bit curious, though I don't like to say it about my blood cousin. She's too fond of a story. She'd have that all around Connacht in no time, trotting in and out of all the houses, puffing it out of her till the fall of night. But she has a grandson and he often does a little message for me. He comes to visit me here sometimes, too. He was supposed to be named Colman, after myself, and that's what he would be but for his father, a contrary man that always wanted to be different from everyone else. Signs on him, he went away on a grain ship and got drowned. That's what happened to him— and it's what always happens to the like of those people."

"What is the boy's name?" I asked.

"A good enough name, I suppose," he said grudgingly. "It's Ciarán, after the great Saint Ciarán, that had the monastery in Clonmacnoise and I suppose he was a better man than me. He's an obliging sort of a boy, and he can hop from one place to another as fast as a swallow. 'You can leave it to me,' he said when I told him what I wanted. 'I'll make out that I have to go to Maas about lobsters.' So he told the grandmother that he would be back tomorrow and off with him. I saw him a short while after, taking the young horse out of the field and galloping off. He said he'd stay the night with a cousin of ours in Carna, maybe, if there's no one in Rossmore that will give him a bed."

"Of course they'll give him a bed," we said indignantly.

For a moment the thought of a strange boy occupying my bed filled me with homesickness. Still, I knew that I had no wish to go home, until I would have seen the end of Sarah's story.

"Ciarán will come over in his own currach tomorrow or after, and tell us how he fared," Colman said. "He's a fine, independent boy, not having any father to chase him, I suppose."

Everything that Colman had said about Ciarán seemed to show that he would deliver his message in the best possible way, and without revealing where we were. Still, it seemed to us that we should waste no time in getting started on our new voyage. A search party might be organized for us, or the

Guards might be asked to find us. A chance visitor to the island might see us, and within hours the rumor of where we were would begin to spread. We did not fear the visitor who had come to the island in the afternoon. We felt sure that he would not want to tell that he had been on Flaherty's Island himself.

All of this we discussed very quietly as we got into bed. It was a warm, still night, and the only sound that reached us was the far-off wash of the waves on the shore. I felt a great pity for old Colman Flaherty, utterly alone in this desolate place, winter and summer, for years and years. At that hour of the night, it was easy to imagine what courage he had needed to stay here. I could not help admiring this courage, though I knew it was well supported by stubbornness and hatred.

In the morning, Colman roused us early. His solicitude for us as unfortunate shipwrecked sailors seemed to have vanished.

"Up out of that, lazybones!" was his first greeting. "Seven o'clock is no time to be lying in bed. If this is the time they get up in Rossmore, it's no wonder ye're all pulling the devil by the tail over there. Up out of that! By the time ye get home, maybe ye'll have learned a few good habits in the islands!"

Furious at these insults, we got up, trying to look as if this were our usual time. Our fathers were always up much earlier, of course, but in Rossmore the people had an idea that boys need plenty of sleep. Time enough to wake us early when we would be full grown, they thought.

I need not say that we did not explain this to Colman. We dressed quickly and helped him to do the necessary things of the house—milking, carrying water, feeding the pigs and the hens. He left most of this to us while he prepared the materials for mending the boat. I took a great interest in these because the thought had occurred to me that if Colman were not a very expert shipwright, his repair might not last quite long enough to bring us to Commillas. As I watched him, however, it seemed to me that he knew exactly what he was doing. It was not only that he had bought some well-seasoned timber, and new screws and nails. What impressed me most was the snarling, impatient expression he wore, which was a replica of my grandfather's when the fever of building the *Santa Maria* was on him.

We had scarcely finished our breakfast when he was calling out:

"Come on, come on! Eat, eat, eat all day! That's always the way with boys." He stopped and said: "Sure, I don't mean a word of it—'tis only the hurry is on me to get on with the boat. Eat up plenty. There's no one ever came to this house that didn't go away with a stomach like a young calf that would be left in with the cows. No hurry at all—I'll wait for ye outside. Eat up, eat up."

And he went outside and sat on the big stone by the door, in the morning sun. We swallowed our last bites and followed him, assuring him that we had had our fill. He sprang up at once and said impatiently:

"What are we waiting for, so? One of ye take the timber. I'll take the tools myself—never trust boys with tools."

And he stumped off down the lane. We followed him at a little distance. After a moment Jim said softly:

"I think I know why all those boys of his went to America. I'm getting anxious myself for our voyage to begin. Did you ever in your life see such a cranky old rasper, such a——"

I poked him into silence, lest Colman might hear us. If he had, I felt sure he would be astonished. It was quite clear to me that he never thought of injuring anyone. He simply behaved as he thought the father of a family should do, or perhaps an army general. Boys and privates were not supposed to have any feelings to be hurt, that was all.

When we rounded the turn of the path, there was the

Santa Maria waiting for us. She looked at ease, as if she were enjoying a rest. The tide was well out, and had still farther to go before the turn. It was a silky smooth sea, reflecting the greenish morning sky. Over its polished surface, sea gulls skimmed along and then landed delicately, leaving a widening circle all around them. The long fingers of rock were baking in the heat, and the orange-colored weed that grew on them glowed like flame.

77

With a fine-bladed saw, Colman set about cutting away the damaged timber, where the boat had struck. He would not allow us to touch anything, except when he shouted to us to hand him one tool or another. He worked as deftly as a woman patching a shirt. We watched him for a while, and then I thought that we might spend our time usefully in cleaning the inside of the boat. But I had no sooner put my foot on her to climb aboard than the old fellow yelled at me so fiercely that I thought he would explode with the force of his own fury:

"Get off that boat! Have ye no sense at all? By the sea gods of ancient Greece, if you shift that boat one inch while I'm working on her——"

He stopped suddenly and seemed to control himself with a great effort. Then he said more kindly:

"Let the two of ye go down to the sea and have a swim. There's only work for one pair of hands on this boat and it makes me mad to see ye idle. Go on down and have a swim. Wait!" He clawed at his tattered pockets and hauled out an ancient piece of string with a hook on the end of it. "Maybe ye'd find an old rockfish below. Sometimes they're stuck in the pools when the tide goes down. Don't be satisfied with a small one—I like my rockfish fat."

You may be sure that we were pleased with this. We took the line and went down to the sea. Where the sand was soft and warm from the sun, we dug up some worms for bait. Jim said:

"Will we swim first or fish first?"

"We'll fish first," I said, "and if we don't catch anything, we'll fish after as well."

"There's no doubt but you have a great brain," said Jim.

I chased him over the rocks, until I saw him stop to stare into a deep pool that had been left behind by the sea. I came up with him and stared too. It was like a little sea, with waving weed and shells and soft, juicy-looking, dark-red anemones clinging to its rocky edges. Sheltering from the sun under the weed, silent and still, there were several rockfish. Only their tails showed, moving as slowly as a fern in a summer breeze.

We baited the hook and let it down gently in front of the nose of the biggest fish. It went down softly, turning a little with the movement of the water. Jim's hand was steadier than mine, as we both knew, so it was he who held the line. I watched without moving, hoping that our shadows lying on the water had not made the fish uneasy. Nothing happened for a while. Jim rolled the string in his fingers to make the bait move. The fish's tail stopped waving and quivered a little. Then it made a sudden flashing dart and snapped at the bait. A second later it was flying through the air, glittering in the sunlight.

Jim was so pleased with his success that he wanted to stay and catch all the other fish as well, but I would not tolerate this.

"If you catch any more of them," I said, "we'll be living on rockfish until we leave Flaherty's Island. And after today, with this heat, they won't be any too fresh. I'd advise you to leave the rest of them where they are—Colman only asked for one, anyway."

Jim saw that there was wisdom in this. We carried our fish down to the edge of the sea and covered it with our clothes while we went in for a swim. Otherwise the sea gulls would have thought that it was a present for themselves.

The sea was sharply cold. We splashed and swam and dived and leaped about like porpoises. There was a little strip of sand bared by the low tide, and we lay on it and drank in the sun, and went back into the sea again to get clean. At last we dressed, and then we sat on the rocks for a long time, unwilling to go back to the old man.

The sun was directly above us when we moved at last. The tide was flowing, and we walked along a rocky reef until we came level with the *Santa Maria*. Already her keel was awash. Colman was standing ankle deep in the water, tapping at his patch with the hammer. It shone starkly white, as neat a piece of work as we had ever seen in our lives. We admired it loudly.

" 'Tis a good job, for sure," he said with satisfaction. "All it needs now is a lick of paint. We'll do that when the tide goes down again."

We gathered up the tools and started for home. Jim and I walked wearily, as if we had been working hard all morning. The rockfish seemed to weigh as much as a lamb. We passed it from one to the other, taking turns with the carrying of it, until Colman said impatiently:

"What kind of grannies are the two of ye? In my young days——"

And he started off on a long account of the hardships he had been accustomed to endure. We began to feel very small, but there was no doubt that our long swim in the sea had wearied us at least as much as any of those marathon trips that he described would have done. I had always found it so, and do to this day.

Back at the house, we fried the fish and ate it with soda-bread and goat's milk. As we sat half-dozing by the fire afterwards, Colman said:

"Tomorrow ye can start off for Spain."

Jim said casually:

"We were thinking you had better come with us. If we go alone, who knows if we'll ever reach Spain at all? 'Tis true we have the sun and the stars to guide us, but Spain is a long way off and if we made a mistake we might strike land in the Canary Islands."

Colman was glaring angrily during this speech. Suddenly he burst out:

"Is it me to go to Spain? To meet that godless thief that took away my daughter? To shake hands with him, maybe?

I thought you told me you are able to navigate a boat. I see now it was all a trick, to get me to patch up the *Santa Maria* for you. Boys are always the same, full of plots and plans for fooling the people——"

I stood up and said furiously:

"We'll be going home, then. I've had enough of this. All morning long you're throwing abuse and insults at us and at all belonging to us. What do we care about Sarah? We were going to risk our necks for your sake, to go to Commillas, where you say yourself the people are godless thieves——"

"For your boat! It's for your boat you were going, to settle her good name. You said it yourself, the first day——"

"We don't have to go to Spain to do that," I said, a little more calmly. "It would be enough for us to go to Aran and back, and the people would see that she's a good boat. We were wanting to help you, to make a try at getting your daughter to come back to you for a visit, but I can see now it would be better to let well alone. You'd only insult her and her husband as you insulted us. Why should we bring the poor woman home to such treatment?"

"I would not! I would not!" He was prancing on his chair with rage. "I'd treat her right, the way I always did."

"If you always treated her right, why didn't she tell you when she was wanting to marry the Spaniard?"

I could feel Jim pulling at my jersey from behind, warning me to be careful. Colman leaped to his feet and roared:

"Because she knew what I'd say——"

He stopped, and dropped back into his chair so suddenly that I thought for a moment that he had had a stroke. His shocked look added to this impression. I put out my hand and touched him. With a quick movement he grasped my hand and shook it, squeezing it painfully tight. Then he said in a croaking, earnest voice which we had not heard him use before:

" 'Tis true for you. 'Tis true for you, indeed. She was

afraid of me. I suppose they were all afraid of me. But sure, what could I do? Someone has to be the head of the family." He was beginning to recover his courage . . . "A father that's soft and easy-going might as well not be there at all. A granny would do as well. You talk fine and soft now because you're a boy, but just wait until you're the father of a family yourself. Then you'll be on the other side of the fence."

It was on the tip of my tongue to say that at least I would be sure not to drive all my family away from me, but I had suddenly lost all wish to try to improve old Colman Flaherty. It seemed to me that it had been left until too late. When I had threatened not to bring Sarah back to him, I had hardly meant it seriously. Now, however, I found that I had come to believe that it would be cruel to bring her all the way back, if she were to face a storm of reproaches as soon as she landed.

It took all afternoon for Colman to persuade me to change my mind. Jim kept out of it. Later he told me that I had been doing so well that he would not have dreamed of interfering. He said he knew the full effect of our long argument would be that the old man would swear to behave well when Sarah would come, and that the fear of being accused again by me would stop him from attacking her.

Of one thing I became quite certain as the afternoon went on: that it would be a torment to be cooped up on the *Santa Maria* for days and days with old Colman. Charity surely would not ask for this. But how were we to get to Commillas without him? He had a compass, he said, and we both knew enough to be able to use it. It was not quite true to say that there was a danger of our ending up in the Canary Islands. The real trouble was that we needed three people on the boat to be sure of not perishing on the way.

Fortunately for us, he did not really want to come.

"God be with the youth of me," he said. "I'd have gone around the world once, and never looked behind me. But old age is a queer, stiff kind of a time. You tell your legs to do this or that, and they just won't obey you. And I get tired now. I never used to get tired."

I remembered the agility with which he had sprung down the path to the sea, and the early hour of the morning at which he always got out of bed. If he was even more energetic when he was young, he must have been a heartscald to live with, I thought, like a baby that doesn't sleep enough.

It was late in the evening before we came to a solution of the problem. We had visited the *Santa Maria* again at the high tide, and had seen her floating as neatly as if she had never had a day's trouble in her life. She still had a slight list from her displaced ballast, but she looked somehow healthier than she had done before. We had put on more bacon to cook, with cabbage. This seemed to be Colman's usual diet except for an occasional pensioner hen. We had milked the goats and fed the pigs. We had collected the eggs and shut in the hens where the fox could not get at them. Just as we sat down to eat at the kitchen table, without warning Ciarán appeared at the door.

We guessed at once who he was. He had come up to the house so quietly that none of us had heard him. Everything he did was quiet. He was taller than either of us, and fair-haired, with the almost white hair that some of the Connemara people have. It was bleached even whiter by the sun, and the darkly tanned skin of his face looked odd by contrast. He wore homespun trousers, like ourselves, and a white knitted jersey with an intricate pattern of trellises and cables and blackberries, which proved that he had an industrious woman to look after him. His voice was soft and low, with a little drawl in it. I never saw the boy hurry at anything he did.

"I came over to tell ye how I got on," he said, "and I have other reasons too. Have ye enough of the bacon to give me a bite?"

Colman put him sitting at the table at once, and cut him two slices of bacon. Ciarán said:

"I came over to have a look at the two visitors, too. I got kind of curious about them."

"Did you see my father?" I asked anxiously.

"I did. First I saw your aunt Maggie, as Colman told me to do."

This was very clever, and I wondered why I had not thought of it myself. Maggie would appreciate our reasons for not wanting to go home at once. But Colman was saying:

"You saw his father! I told you not to do that. They'll be after ye like a dog after a rabbit. Why didn't you do what you were told?"

"Wait a bit and you'll hear. If you only wanted someone to do what he was told, why did you pick on me to send?"

" 'Tis true for you. Go on with your story."

"I told Maggie, as I said, that the boys are safe but that they have some business to do and they won't be back for a few weeks, maybe. Then I stayed inside in Maggie's house, resting myself, while she went off to tell the fathers. I'd left the horse a piece outside Rossmore, the way the people wouldn't all be watching me go in to Maggie's house."

"Good boy, good boy. What happened then?"

"Maggie was gone a long time, near on two hours. When she came back into the house, I knew right off that something was wrong. Do you know what they said to her?"

"No, no. Go on, go on!" said Colman, but I had begun to guess.

"They were very nice to her, she said. They knew how she felt because herself and everyone in the village has been lamenting the boys for two days back. They didn't say she was telling lies. They didn't say she was making it all up. They said she was imagining it, because of herself and her father having built the boat, and because she didn't want to face the truth. I never saw such a look on a woman's face as long as I'm alive. She didn't know whether to be raging mad or to cry, or maybe even to believe them. She asked me to tell my story again and again until she was sure it was true. Of course she asked me had I seen the boys, and I had to tell her no, but that they were staying in a safe place. And then she made me promise to come over and see them for myself. And there's still another reason why I'm here."

"Yes, yes. Tell it, tell it for the love of heaven!"

"Can I have a bite of my dinner first? The smell of it is driving me mad."

"Take a bite, so."

We watched the bite go in. It seemed to take an age. When he could speak again Ciarán said:

"We talked about it for a while, and then we agreed that the only thing to be done was for me to tell the story myself to the fathers of the two boys. I wouldn't go to their houses, because someone might recognize me on the way. They're terrible travelers in Rossmore. There's no knowing but one of them might have seen me in Carraroe, or in Maas with the lobsters. So Maggie locked me into the house again and went off and fetched the men down to see me. I told them the same story as I had told Maggie. They had come down just to humor her, but they believed me, all right. Then they began to question me. Where was I from? Who were my people? How had I got to Rossmore? Above all, where were their two sons? I wouldn't answer anything, only saying they were safe, they'd be home soon—all that class of thing. Then I saw one of them getting ready to make a drive at me. I was thinking, if they caught me, they might squeeze the truth out of me. I didn't wait for that. I pelted out of the door and away down to the sea and up the stream under the bridge, and out of the village, until I got back to where my horse was. I'm telling you we knocked sparks out of the road home. And now I want another few bites of my dinner. I'll be telling you more afterwards."

(6)

From the way that Ciarán attended to his dinner, we could see that it would be no use questioning him any further for a while. In any case we had suddenly become ravenously hungry ourselves. We had a great deal of thinking to do, and there is no better help to thought than a good dinner. At last we moved across to the fire again and Ciarán said what was in all our minds:

"I can't go back to Carraroe for a while."

" 'Tis true for you," said Colman. "You can stay here with me. I could use a boy around the place."

A look came over Ciarán's face like the look of a trapped badger. His eyes darted quickly to the door, almost as if he thought of making a run for it immediately. It appeared that he knew Colman at least as well as we did.

"Much better for him to come with us," I said firmly. "We need a third man, as we were saying. If he's with us, no one will find him. It could happen that the Rossmore people would think of looking for us in the islands, and if they found Ciarán here, they wouldn't be long putting two and two together."

I wondered why Colman was giving me such fierce looks during this speech. I had expected him to be pleased, firstly to be relieved of the need for coming with us himself and also because I had not really believed that he wanted to have the task of hiding Ciarán until our return.

"Come with you! Come with you! Why don't you tell it to the whole world, put it in the newspapers, maybe? Now you've said so much, he'll be able to guess the rest."

"But Colman, surely you know you couldn't keep a secret like that!"

"I suppose I couldn't keep it secret forever," Colman said, "but the longer I can keep it, the better I like it. There's them in Carraroe, aye, and farther away too, that would like the satisfaction of it if she wouldn't come. Had you thought of that?"

I had not thought of it, and now I saw there was a great risk that Sarah would refuse to come to Ireland ever again. The humiliation of old Colman would be great, indeed, if this were to happen.

Ciarán was looking at us curiously. Now he said to Colman:

"You ought to know by now that I don't talk. What about all the little messages I've done for you in my day, that if they were known would cause you trouble enough? And if you don't trust me any more, where are you going to find another messenger?"

He said this very quietly and reasonably, but I could see that he was anxious enough to know what our secret was.

"Did you ever hear of my daughter Sarah?" Colman asked after a pause.

"The one that's in Spain, married to a trawlerman? I did, of course. Isn't she a cousin of my own too?"

"Everyone has heard of Sarah," Colman said bitterly. "Some of them know more about her than I know myself. She's gone from me twenty years this month. We had a plan— a plan." He stopped, and a moment later he burst out: "You tell it. Tell him our plan!"

And suddenly he was gone out of the house, crashing the half-door shut behind him.

We were embarrassed for him, almost as if he had been a relation whose manners had failed in the presence of visitors. Then Ciarán said:

"Now tell me, before he comes back, or I'll die of curiosity. Are you planning to go for Sarah and bring her back with you?"

"Right first time," said Jim with respect. "How did you guess?"

"You left out enough hints. And besides I've had the idea for a long time myself. Over in Carraroe, whenever old Colman comes for his groceries, they talk about him for half a day after—what a terrible thing it is for him to be here alone, how he never sees the daughter that's married right near him, nor the other one that went to Spain and never came back. Many a time I thought of going on one of the Spanish trawlers that go to her place, to ask her to come back, but I never did it."

"Why not?"

"I was afraid, I suppose. 'Tis a long way to go. And I thought that when I'd get there, perhaps Sarah wouldn't listen to me and I'd have my journey for nothing. Maybe she won't listen to you either."

"True enough," I said. "Why should she listen to us? That was why we thought of bringing her father to her instead. But he doesn't want to come."

"Thanks be to God!" said Jim.

"He's goodhearted, though," Ciarán said. "His bark is worse than his bite. You have to know him well."

"Do you think he'll be civil to Sarah if he sees her again?"

"He will. My grandmother says he has learned a few things in his lifetime. She says that only a few months ago he was telling her that if he had all his children back again, he would be sure to treat them in a different way."

I almost blushed to think of how I had lectured Colman that very afternoon, on how to treat his family. Then I remembered that his manners to ourselves had not been very gentle, especially after the first day. I wondered if even with the best of intentions he would be able to stand the strain of being polite to his daughter for long.

Our conversation was cut short by the appearance of the old man again. Leaning on the half-door, blacking out the fading daylight, he looked like an ancient wizard with his wild white hair and face like a last-year's chestnut.

"Well, will you go?" he challenged Ciarán at once.

"Oh, yes, I'll go," Ciarán said in his quiet drawl. "I was in Brittany several times," he explained to us. "I went with a Carraroe man that goes there sometimes for the tunny fishing and the sardines. You'll have to tell my grandmother," he said to Colman.

"I'll go tonight. It will be well to do it after darkness falls, so that the Carraroe people won't see me coming nor going. That way there won't be any questions."

"Will you tell her where we're going?" Colman asked mischievously.

Colman gave a kind of hoot.

"Is it Sabina? I'll tell that one nothing. I'll say you're spending a few days with me to keep off the lonesomeness and to do a bit of painting. She'll be glad enough, because she's always hoping I'll leave you the island when I die. Ever since the time when I got the pneumonia last year, it's plain to be seen in her eye. That's why she never complains when you go for my messages."

I thought that Ciarán would be embarrassed at this, but he was quite unconcerned. Indeed, I have never known anyone like him for keeping his head in the midst of surprises. Perhaps he had had a great many of them. He just smiled gently and said:

"Yes, tell her that. Maybe I'll do a bit of painting for you too, to make it true."

When it was almost dark, we went down to the beach with Colman to see him off to Carraroe. The last of the sunset had turned the sea a reddish gold, so that it looked like polished copper. A huge moon was rising, strongly colored and brilliant. Colman's currach slid off almost without a sound, as he dipped his narrow-bladed oars into the silent sea.

We carried Ciarán's currach up to the top of the beach and hid it in a deep dike where there were brambles and long grasses to cut it off from view. In that place it would also be safe from the wind, which is the greatest hazard with boats as light as ours.

"It may be there for a long time," Ciarán said. "Cover it well."

This simple remark brought a sudden unwelcome thought into my mind: that the currach might lie there forever, if we did not come back at all.

Colman would certainly be gone for three hours. There was nothing we could do, now that darkness had fallen, but go back to the house and start the fire blazing and settle down to talk about our voyage. It soon turned out that from his voyages to Brittany, Ciarán had a very good idea of what stores we would need and of the length of time it would take to reach the north coast of Spain. It would be almost twice as long as the journey to Brittany, he had heard the men say—perhaps seven hundred miles or so. Even with fair winds all the way, it could not be done in a week. We would have to hug the coast all the way, he said, because the sea between France and Spain was noted for sudden storms. I found that this prospect did not frighten me. I knew how the *Santa Maria* behaved in a storm, and I thought it unlikely that we would come upon anything worse than the one we had experienced on our way to Flaherty's Island.

It was midnight when Colman returned. We had gone down to the strand to watch out for him. It was a clear night with the moon, now pale, high overhead. Away off on the coast the lights of Carraroe shone faintly. Over to the right of us the Inishownan lights were clearer. We found a hollow like a huge nest under a bank of grass, and huddled together in there from the night breeze.

"There he is," Ciarán said after a long time.

Sure enough, a slow black shadow was stealing toward us. I would not let the others run down to the shore until we were sure that it was Colman.

"It might be that same sneaking visitor," I said.

Ciarán asked at once:

"What visitor?"

We told him of the man we had seen enter Colman's house while he was in Carraroe, and of how he had run off like a thief when we had appeared.

"Perhaps you know who he is," Jim said.

Ciarán made us describe the man closely. Then he said:

"It's time Sarah came home, all right."

When Colman was close in, we went down onto the beach to help him to come ashore. He was in high good humor. Sabina had treated him with unprecedented hospitality—currant cake and butter, and as much buttermilk and poiteen as he could handle. He kept on giving little hoots of amusement as he remembered it.

"She thinks now that you're certain of the island," he said to Ciarán. "There she was, filling my glass as often as I'd take a sup out of it, and do you know what I thought?"

"What did you think?"

"That it was like as if she was celebrating my wake. She was as happy as a child with a bag of sweets." He broke into what he clearly thought was an imitation of the cracked voice of an old woman, but it was not very different from his own usual one. " 'Of course you can keep him as long as you like,'

92

she says. 'I'll manage along somehow. The neighbors are very good, thanks be to God. And sure you need him more than I do, and you out there in that lonesome place and no one to say a word to you from morning till night.' "

"Maybe she meant that," I protested, not liking to see the poor woman's motives estimated so low.

"She did not, then," Colman said positively. "I know Sabina well. I took a rise out of her then. I said to her: ' 'Tis true for you, Sabina, he might be lonesome on the island all right. 'Twould take a woman to think of that, so it would.' Well, she was in a fit then, not knowing what to say. I thought she'd fall over her tongue in her hurry to tell me what a brave boy Ciarán is, and that he's not afraid of hog, dog, nor devil. 'Maybe I will keep him for a good while, so,' said I, thinking to myself that we don't know how long that voyage is going to take. And I was thinking too that when ye come back, maybe I'll get my painting done as well, as we were saying, and we could be having good times here together with no one to give us orders."

Ciarán smiled gently and said:

"That would be a great life."

Knowing how little he would have enjoyed living here alone with the old man, I was astonished at his apparent acceptance of the idea. He was always like that, never fussing or worrying in advance but just dealing with each problem as it came along. He slept in our room that night, in the huge bed where there was room for the three of us. He slept like a baby, long before we did, seeming quite undisturbed by the thought of our coming adventure.

In the morning we took Ciarán to have a look at the *Santa Maria*. The old man stayed at home to bake bread for our voyage. As usual we were relieved to be rid of his company for a while. We spent the morning in fixing up a brazier for cooking in the little cabin and in stacking some turf on board. The brazier was an old galvanized iron bucket punched all over with holes. It stood on two flat stones with a space between to let in the air. While it was in use, it would be placed directly under the hatchway, which would serve fine as a chimney. An old tin under it would catch most of the ashes. With a wooden boat I suppose there was some danger that we would burn a hole in the bottom, but turf is not nearly as hot as coal and I have never known one of these braziers to start a fire.

"We'll have to put out the fire every time we're finished with the cooking anyway," Ciarán said, "to save turf and not to have the cabin full of smoke. An oil stove would be good, maybe, but those things sometimes explode and then we'd be in the height of trouble."

As he seemed so experienced, we elected him the cook and fireman. We would need fishing lines, he said, and a couple of sharp knives to gut the fish with. We would eat fish whenever we could catch some because it was quick to cook and it would save our storage space. Eggs are tidy things, he said, and they fill you up like meat. Of course we would have a sack of potatoes and Colman's loaves of bread to fill any remaining spaces. It sounded fine.

"We won't starve, anyway," I said comfortably.

"Not unless we run off our course," said Ciarán. "Some of the Carraroe men say they once came on a drifting hooker and a dead man in it, that had died of starvation. Of course he was not a Connemara man," he added hastily, seeing our expressions. "He was from Kerry. He must have been lost for a long time, the men said, until the boat drifted up this way. He must have had another man with him in the beginning, because no one goes in a hooker alone if he can help it, but they never found trace of any but the one."

I did not like that story and I wished he had not told it.

"If you have any more stories like that," I said, "just keep them bottled up inside you until we're safe home again.

That's not the kind of entertainment we want on the voyage."

He laughed and promised that he would tell no more of them. Something in the way he said this suggested that he had a few more in store, that he could have told if he liked.

After dinner we brought down the two sacks of straw which were to serve us as mattresses. The cabin would hold no more than two, and in any case we knew that we should never be able to sleep all at the same time. In the shelter of the cabin, we put two little barrels of fresh water. We brought a pot for potatoes, and a frying pan, three tin plates and some knives, a little canister of tea which we would drink black with sugar, and a piece of Colman's bacon.

"But we won't have time to cook that bacon," Ciarán said. "It takes too long to boil it."

"Then you can slash the fat off it to cook your fish," said Colman. "I'm telling you, when you're eating fish for a week, you'll be praying for me and my bacon."

Colman looked twice his age this evening. He had spent the day at the bread-making—as much time as he could spare from his most necessary tasks outside. He had a little stack of loaves ready and a box full of eggs. He had been saving these for a day or two, and he had also taken a present of some from Sabina.

"Every time I visit her she offers me a few eggs and I going away," he said. "I always tell her I have eggs in plenty at home, but this time I said I'd take them and be thankful. You should have seen her face! I think she thought her last hour was on her, but she gave them to me just the same."

All evening, every time he thought of Sabina he chuckled and made some little remark about how he had taken her at her word about the eggs.

We had planned to go at the dawn, so as not to be noticed.

"Oh, they'll see you going, all right," Colman said. "At least, some one contrary man that ought to be home in bed will see the boat pulling out and he'll say to himself: 'Now where is old Colman sneaking off to?' He'll be waiting to ask me all about it, the next time I go over to Carraroe. I'll say 'twas surely a ghost ship he saw."

This notion afforded him great amusement, but I did not care for it. Now that we were ready to go, I had become very uncertain as to whether we had the skill or the wit to find our way to Commillas. As the evening went on, however, we discovered that Ciarán really did know something about navigation. He and Colman had a map, and they planned the whole course inch by inch in a way that I would not have thought possible. Though my father owned a good hooker, he was not an adventurous sailor. He used it only for taking sheep and young cattle to Galway, for he was really mostly occupied with farming. His farthest trip was to Aran with a load of turf, and this he only did during the little gap in May between the planting and the first of the harvest.

Jim understood better than I did what they were doing and after he had made a few intelligent comments, they took him into their counsels. Then they found out that his great-grandfather had sailed the Atlantic with Captain Hennessy. Colman got very excited at this.

"I remember Captain Hennessy when he was an old man," he said. "He had a house in Barna and a grand boat there that he used to take out by himself until he was eighty. When I was a younger man, going in to Galway in my own hooker with maybe one or two of the boys, sometimes we'd pass him and he'd wave to us. They don't make men like that nowadays at all."

We had to drink a little poiteen to celebrate his memory.

It seemed that we had been only an hour in bed when Colman was bawling at the door:

"Up, up! Ye lazy, good-for-nothings! This is no way to start a voyage, lying in bed late. Breakfast in two minutes!"

Ciarán sprang up and asked:

"What time is it?"

"Four o'clock," said the old villain and went off chuckling, knowing that we were wide awake.

We dressed quickly and followed him out to the kitchen. Sure enough, he had breakfast with boiled eggs ready on the table. I went to the door for a few moments before sitting down to eat. It was daylight as it always is in Ireland at that hour on a summer's morning. The grass was heavy with dew and gave off a rich scent. A breeze stirred the leaves of the blackberry bushes in the hedges. The sky was a clear, pale blue, but the sun was not high enough to be visible yet.

"A grand day," old Colman was saying. "Made to measure. Let ye hurry on there now and be gone, while ye have the good breeze. 'Twas God sent us this weather."

We hurried over breakfast and in a few minutes we were on our way to the sea. We were to go out on the ebbing tide. It was a healthy-looking sea, dark blue and with a comfortable number of waves, of the kind you get with the best sailing wind. We had moored the boat by the reef of rocks, in a place that Colman said he sometimes used, where there was deep water at high tide. He came aboard with us to give a last foreman's look at everything. Then he said:

"I'm mighty glad to see this ship here this morning. When ye come back, it would be better to sail around to where I keep my own hooker."

"Why?"

"Because this is a dangerous place to leave a boat," said he calmly. "There's a wind comes in here that would grind her to powder before you could do a thing to save her."

"Why did you let us leave her here, then, all the days we've been with you?"

"Don't flare up at me like that, young fellow! I didn't want your boat to be seen. You weren't anxious for her to be seen either."

I repented immediately of my temper. It was true that we had been anxious to conceal the *Santa Maria*, but now the thought that another storm might have finished her off made me almost taste this misfortune though it had never happened.

The old man climbed ashore and cast off the sheet from the spur of rock to which we were moored. Jim pushed off with his hands on the rock, while I hauled up sail. Ciarán had the helm. We had taken these tasks naturally without any discussion, and so it was throughout our voyage. We cooperated without effort, each doing what had to be done without consulting the others.

The mainsail unrolled and filled with the good breeze. In a moment we were three yards from the rocks and heading for the open sea. We heard Colman call out something but it was carried away on the wind. Then we saw him run along the reef, cross the stony beach and climb the winding path to the cliff-top. For a long time we could see him standing there, waving to us. Jim said:

"I hope he won't stay on top of that cliff until we come back."

"He'll spend a lot of time there, you may be sure," said Ciarán, "but it will be nothing new to him. Ever since Sarah went away, the Carraroe people say they used to see him up there when they would be passing by, as if he were watching for her to come back. Think of it—watching like that for twenty years!"

"What kind of a woman is she?" I asked. "What do the people say about her?"

"They say nothing but good," said Ciarán. "She was a grand woman, and if the old rasper had had an ounce of sense, he could have her spending half the year with him always."

"He didn't like the Spaniard, he said."

"He never laid an eye on that man in his life, the people

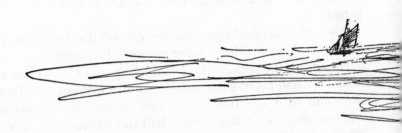

say," said Ciarán. "And he was a decent man and a cheerful one, always singing and dancing, and he played the concertina fit to break your heart. Colman was suspicious of him because he wasn't Irish. Did you ever hear such rubbish? The world knows that Spain was always a good friend of Ireland, sending over soldiers to fight our wars in the bad old times, and dearly they paid for it, if we can believe what we read. The people told Colman all that, but the minute that the Spaniard's name was mentioned, he'd get into such a rage you'd think he'd burn a hole in himself. After a while, everyone gave up reasoning with him."

"He talks as if everything that happened—Sarah's leaving him and all—is a great secret."

"He likes to pretend it's a secret but he knows well enough that you can't keep a secret like that, especially in west Connacht. What else would we be talking about if we didn't have our neighbors' ups and downs?"

Soon the island and the long mountainy coast behind it were dropping into the sea. The *Santa Maria* sailed like a swan, as sweetly as she had done the first day that we had taken her out. She did not feel in the least too small. In fact as time went on a curious change came about in our view of her: she became the whole world to us. It is difficult to ex-

plain this sensation. To a mouse living behind a kitchen wall, it must seem that his nest is the center of the universe, and that it is a most reasonable thing to live by darting out for a few dropped crumbs when the house is quiet and the cat is out.

It was something like this with us. Our ship did not feel small since she was big enough for us. We hardly looked beyond her at the sea around us, except to observe the weather or to do some fishing. After the excitement of starting our voyage, our nights and days slipped into an easy rhythm of sleeping and eating and trimming the sails, following the course that Ciarán knew, and in fishing and cooking our meals.

For long spells we were able to lash the helm and lie back chatting to each other, or sleeping, or fishing. We caught some strange-looking fish and we ate all except one kind, though we had never seen their like before. The one that we rejected was black, and had a head like a sledge hammer and the undercut jaw of a shark. It was Jim that caught it. His yell brought us flying to see it. Then, without a word, he unhooked it and slid it back into the sea again. We were all glad to see it go. Somehow its ugliness had disturbed us. We did not want to know too much about the strange beasts that live on the ocean's floor, I suppose, at least until we were on dry land again.

It was nearly a week before we saw a long, low coastline away off in front of us. All morning long, Ciarán had been gazing at the horizon, refusing to leave the helm even to eat. At noon I brought him a plate of potatoes and some mackerel fried in bacon fat.

"If we're any good, we should see it today," he said. "We've had a fair wind all the way. I wish I knew what our speed is— you can't calculate it so well when you don't know all the currents."

Later in the afternoon, we all saw it.

"It's the French coast," Ciarán said. "There are miles and miles of sandy beaches, down as far as Bordeaux."

We had planned to keep the coast in sight for the rest of the way. I found it a great comfort always to be able to see land. I no longer felt that we might be lost on the ocean and go sailing around and around forever. Several times during the night, I woke up and climbed the ladder from the smoky cabin to enjoy the specks of light that we could see on higher ground.

But one effect of having land in sight was that now we seemed to crawl along where before we had thought we were flying over the sea. Sometimes we saw huge steamers which moved majestically across our view, while we seemed to stay still. Once, one of them saw us and hooted a greeting. Ciarán said that we must keep well away from them, for fear of being run down.

Since we had sighted the land, he had become much more confident. This meant that we were more lighthearted too, because seeing how much more experienced he was, we took our moods from him. Therefore we were completely dismayed one evening to see a look of horror come over his face suddenly as he stood at the helm.

"Look!" He pointed a shaking finger and seemed to fight for breath. "Lower the sail—anyhow! Get it down!"

We gave one glance in the direction where he had pointed and fell on the sheets, bringing the mainsail tumbling down in a heap. What we had seen was a kind of whirling, blackish pillar, spinning toward us across the surface of the sea. It was as if a little bunch of devils was struggling together. Everywhere it passed, the sea swirled in a terrible, white, boiling agony. There was no question of avoiding it, for it seemed to dance here and there over the whole area that lay before us.

"Lie down!" Ciarán said.

We threw ourselves on the deck, huddling under the shelter of the rail in a way that seemed to me futile. The squall looked powerful enough to turn the *Santa Maria* upside down and empty us out into the ocean, like cockles emptied out of a bucket, if it had a mind to.

"*Santa Maria,*" I said in my own mind, "*Santa Maria,* this is your boat. Protect us now, for Colman's sake, for our mothers who will never know what has happened to us. It was for this that my grandfather named her——"

Suddenly we felt the hooker lurch and turn with a horrid plunging movement, as if she were going to nose-dive into the depths. A tall wave looked in at us and then its tip came pouring into the boat. With a second lurch her nose came up like a frightened horse, and we looked for what seemed a long time down into the deadly blackness of the sea. A thought of that hammer-headed fish flashed into my mind but before I could become properly aware of it we were floating evenly again.

The other two looked like ghosts. Their faces were a queer grayish green and their eyes were wild. We were soaked to the skin, yet we lay there in inches of water for a full minute before Ciarán put his head up and said in a voice that shook like an old woman's:

"Look, it's gone."

We lifted our heads too, as cautiously as snails. There was the squall, still spinning and turning its way along the sea, moving farther and farther away from us with every moment.

"Is there any fear it might come back?" I asked.

"No," Ciarán said. "It won't come back. They never do."

(7)

We were very quiet after our escape. We hung our soaked clothes to dry, when we had got the sail up again, and then we got the brazier going and cooked a meal. It was wonderfully comforting. We had become very tired of our diet of fish and potatoes, helped out by Colman's bread, which was rock-hard by now. But all at once, the monotonous food seemed to have taken on a new savor. I think now that it was the savor of life itself.

Though we had not had to fight the squall in any bodily way, still we were tired and depressed after it had gone. I suppose we did not believe what Ciarán had said—that it would not come back. There was a good steady breeze now, of the kind which yesterday had seemed so reliable that we had slept by turns in the afternoon. This evening none of us wanted to lie down. Especially we did not want to go down into the cabin. Though no one said it, for all of us the clearest vision of the squall had been in the moment when the *Santa Maria*'s bows had pointed to the sky and we had gripped the rail in terror of her capsizing. Somehow it seemed more desirable not to be drowned inside the cabin.

We brought up blankets, therefore, and rolled ourselves in them on the deck. The air was warm though evening was coming on. In spite of myself, I slept heavily when my turn came.

During that night, gradually we became easier. Ciarán set a course for us, and he slept too. We were keeping well out from a rough, mountainy coastline, rather like our own. Groups of lights showed early in the night from mountain villages. Later it was all dead black. When morning came, we saw a beautiful range of hills, a little back from the shore. It was not clear at that distance, but it seemed that these hills were greener than ours, as if they were covered with grass and trees instead of with rock and bog as ours were.

Here and there, down by the sea little towns seemed to grow around curving harbors. Each one had a long pier that reached out into the sea. Still we kept far out, though we were all seized with a fierce longing to sail into one of those little ports and feel dry land under our feet again.

"If we were to land now, we'd never see Sarah," Ciarán said when Jim suggested that we put in for an hour.

"We'd put the comether on some old one," Jim said persuasively, "and she'd cook us a fine stew, maybe, or a pot of soup."

"She'd call the police while we'd be eating it," Ciarán said. "We have no right to land in Spain at all, with ne'er a passport among the three of us."

"A passport!" I was astonished. "Do you mean to say that a person has to have a passport to land in a foreign country, even for an hour?"

"I don't know," said Ciarán, "but I wouldn't like to risk it. Or it could happen that some busybody might think we're too young to be sailing alone, and they mightn't let us put to sea again. The best thing is for us to go to Commillas while the going is good. Sarah will look after us when we get there."

Watching those villages and towns from the sea all day long was like one of the trials of Ulysses, I thought. We saw smoke go up from the chimneys in thin, feathery lines at dinnertime, and we began to wonder what the Spaniards over there would be eating.

"Rice," Ciarán said, "with tomatoes and spices, and bits of fish and chicken mixed in with it, and shellfish. My uncle told me that's what he ate in Spain."

"New, fresh bread," I said, "with good thick crust on it the way you'd have some satisfaction in biting into it."

"Soup," said Jim, "with carrots and every other kind of thing in it—the kind of soup that gets better the longer you keep it. A Spanish woman made it once in our house when she came with her husband on the trawler."

Each of us thought for a long time on his favorite food, as if we hoped that this would be as good as eating it. But then we had to hack a piece off the last of old Colman's loaves and soak it in water to make it possible to swallow it at all. Try as I would, I could not make mine taste of spices and chicken and tomatoes.

Toward evening the land became less mountainous. A fine breeze had come up at three o'clock and it sent us flying along steadily before it. The sea was dark blue as far as we could see, with a dark-blue sky above. Out on the horizon there were woolly white clouds, but they seemed to be stationary.

Just as it was getting dark, we began to pass a huge city. Ciarán said that this must be Bilbao, and that it was a great port. We saw big, dirty ships go in and out, puffing jet-black smoke over the sea and the sky. On land, more clouds of smoke flew up in long black lines from tall chimneys. The countryside around the city seemed to have become blackened by all that smoke. It was ugly and yet in some strange way exciting, but I had no inclination to see it any closer. On the map it was marked that a river flowed in there, but we were too far away to see it clearly.

Long after we had passed it, during my watch I could still see a red glow in the sky above Bilbao. Some time during the night, it dropped behind us. When I came up from the cabin

into broad daylight next morning, once more we were passing by quiet green hills.

The pattern of the weather seemed to be much more steady here than in Connemara. With us, a day could begin in summer and end in winter. Here, every morning the breeze was light and the sea calm, so that we did not make much headway. Early every afternoon, however, the wind strengthened to a fine steady blow that never failed until sundown, when again it became lighter. And all the time, the warm sun gladdened our hearts.

"The Spaniards are blessed with their weather," I said.

Jim said:

"I heard my father say that that is why they lose their boats when they come to Irish waters. A trawler that will be safe enough in these waters won't last more than an hour or two in one of our storms."

"But they come so often to Ireland, you'd think they'd know by now that they should have better boats. And what about the squalls they have here? Aren't they dangerous enough to warrant a good boat?"

"They don't think any boat will stand up to them," Jim said. "And they just run for shelter from our storms. No more than ourselves, I don't think they can afford any better boats. How is a poor man going to buy a new boat, or even to mend his old one, with the profit from fishing?"

It seemed to us a great injustice that a man's life should be in danger, merely for want of money, and yet we knew that the whole world was run like that.

A clean, white city on the edge of the sea was identified by Ciarán from the map as Santander. After it, we sailed closer in, past hills covered with purple-flowering trees, past long, white strands, and past many white-walled villages. On a quiet, sunny morning, we came at last to Commillas.

The quay was so like our own that the dark faces looking down at us were a surprise, and especially the strange language. It was easy to find a place to tie up by the long stone steps among the fishing boats. We threw a rope ashore and saw it seized and made fast by a boy of our own age. There were several men with soft, drawling voices, a little like the voices of the Aranmen. They craned over the quay wall and read the name of our boat aloud. Then one called out to us in Spanish. Ciarán said:

"Is this Commillas?"

"Sí, sí! Commillas!"

All the heads were nodding, and then one man was pushed forward by several of the others. He hung back against the others, and I saw that he was blushing with shyness. He looked gravely down into the boat and said slowly in English:

"You are very welcome to Commillas. Do you come from Ireland?"

"Yes, yes. From Rossmore in Connemara."

This information was passed on. We could hear exclamations of interest. We waited for no more but climbed ashore and started up the steps to the quay.

Just like the excitement of putting to sea, the excitement of landing was deep and powerful. The steps seemed to rock under our feet with the motion of the boat, so that I clutched the wall to prevent myself from pitching into the sea. There was a soft laugh from above us, quickly stifled from politeness. The man who spoke English said:

"You have been a long time at sea if you have come from Ireland. Is there no man with you?"

"No. We are good enough sailors."

"So you must be, to have come alone."

He looked us over, his black eyes dancing with curiosity, obviously longing to ask what had brought us. Already he must have guessed that it was no accident, since we had known the name of the village.

We said no more until we were all safely on the quay. At one side there was a curving strand with a reef of rocks beyond. The sand seemed as white and fine as sugar. Behind it there were grassy hills, with big white houses. At the other side of the quay, we could see the red roofs of the little town. It seemed to me that a heavenly smell rose up from it, of all the most appetizing foods in the world. I do not know whether we all pointed our noses to the sky and howled, but it certainly happened that the men looked at us anxiously and huddled together, and then the English speaker said:

"We would like you to eat soon. If you come from Ireland you are hungry—it is a long way."

He seemed almost apologetic about offering us a meal. You may be sure that we were not long in accepting, though we tried to do so politely, without showing the real size of our appetites. As we all went up the quay together, I thought that our mothers would have been proud of us then. We wanted to run ahead, to follow those delicious smells home to their own kitchens and to sniff around the pots while the cooking finished. Instead we moved at a decent pace, answering questions and waiting while the answers were translated into Spanish for the benefit of the people who did not understand English.

Our interpreter's name was Alonso. He often went to Ireland, he said, but always to the south, to Kinsale and Bantry and Valentia. He had many friends in those places, and to talk to them he had had to learn English.

"But we do not often have an Irish visitor in Commillas," he said. "The Irish boats are smaller and, besides, the fish are more plentiful around the Irish coast so there is no need for the men to go far away." He looked at us sideways. "We have never before had an Irish hooker tied up to our quay at Commillas."

"You saw the name of our boat?" I said.

"Yes, yes. A Spanish name."

"*Santa Maria.* It was my grandfather's choice of a name for this boat. He built her, and perhaps he knew she would go to Spain some day."

"He will be happy to know she has come safely."

"If he could have known it—but he is dead."

"So you took the hooker for a cruise to Spain to please his wandering spirit, perhaps?"

"In a way. We had another reason, too," Ciarán said. "We came to look for a woman called Sarah Flaherty. She is married to a Spaniard in Commillas——"

"Ah, Sarah! We wondered how you knew the name of our village. It is not a big place like Vigo or Santander or Bilbao."

He spent a few minutes in translating for his friends while we waited. A great fear had been on me for days past, that we would arrive to find that Sarah was dead, or that she had left Commillas. I had said nothing of it to the others—indeed I had been afraid even to think it clearly to myself. Now I felt that the way he had said her name proved that she was alive and well, and so it turned out to be. When he turned back to us again, he said:

"I can take you to Sarah. And she will give you food, for certain."

Still he curbed his curiosity. Such courtesy was astonishing, I thought. I had often observed the same in the men of Rossmore and had wondered if I could ever hope to achieve it myself.

The village was beautifully placed, in a sheltered hollow that seemed specially made to protect it. To get there we had to climb a little hill and then go down at the other side by a winding road. Everywhere there were flowers, bigger and more strongly colored than any we had ever seen before. We passed some farmhouses—strong, comfortable buildings with plenty of fine sheds all around them. At the edge of the village we saw something that seemed to us very strange: a great trough had been built of stone, with a wide stone rim all around it. A number of women were there with baskets of washing which they were pounding and scrubbing and rinsing in the trough. While they worked, they laughed and talked noisily. I thought what a good idea it was, and wondered if we could have something of the kind in Rossmore. It looked so much more cheerful to have everyone working together.

But almost at once I began to think of what my mother would say to this idea. She had a favorite proverb: "Where there's smoke, there's a fire; where there's a fire, there are women; where there are women, there's gossip." She would think it was tempting providence to have all the women gathering regularly for such a common task as washing. Also, I could imagine how she would not care to wash any but the newest and best clothes under the eyes of the other women.

While we watched, the women lifted their baskets full of washing onto their heads, where they balanced them perfectly. Then they set off up the street with them, toward the village. The women who sell fish in Galway always carry their baskets on their heads but theirs is a flat, light load compared with this. Yet these women walked as straight as a ship's mast, apparently quite unconcerned.

We followed them and soon came to a little square. It was shaded from the sun by spreading trees under which there were benches with people resting on them. All around there were tall houses with shutters on every window. I remember thinking that here surely lived the richest people in the town, but then Alonso led us straight to one of the wide, beautiful doorways and called out in English:

"Sarah! Sarah! Some friends from Ireland to see you!"

As long as I live, I can never forget my first sight of Sarah. She came out of the kitchen at the end of the hallway. She was carrying a long wooden spoon with which she had been stirring a sauce. The neatest woman in the whole world, still she dropped that spoon with a clatter on the tiled floor and stood there, with her arms hanging at her sides and a look of astonishment on her face.

You can imagine with what interest we gazed back at her. She was a tall woman and black-haired, thin and straight as so many of our people are. Her skin was darkened by the sun and she wore her hair as the Spanish women did, parted in the middle and rolled into a huge bun at the back of her neck. Yet I think I would have known her anywhere for an Irishwoman. Her eyes were sharper and more blue, and her expression had more strength and determination in it than her easygoing neighbors'.

Then we saw that she looked disappointed. It was not surprising. Alonso had said we were friends from Ireland. Perhaps she had hoped to see her father or one of her brothers. Three strange boys, none too clean, must have looked less interesting. Then Ciarán said:

"Sarah! I'm your cousin Ciarán—my grandmother is Sabina Flaherty."

"Sabina is still alive?" she said softly.

"Alive and kicking," said Ciarán, "but she doesn't know I'm here. Only your father knows that."

"My father!"

"Yes. He sent us."

It was not hard to see the relief in her face at this. Now I guessed she must have thought that the only thing that would have brought us to visit her would be the news of her father's death. Quickly I said:

"He helped us to get the boat ready. He can climb the cliff path a lot faster than we can. He can row his currach over to Carraroe and back, twice in one day if he wants to. His house is like a new pin, with clean whitewash and delft on the dresser, and roses around the door. It's all spick and span, he says, waiting for the day——"

"What day?" she asked as I stopped.

"The day when Sarah comes home."

She stared at me so long that I thought I had offended her terribly. We stood there, looking back at her for what seemed like a long time. The smell of her sauce came pouring out of the kitchen behind her, filling the air all around us. I felt almost faint with longing for it. I said:

"Perhaps it will burn."

The light seemed to spring back into her eyes, which had gone quite still. She whirled around and ran back into the kitchen. Ciarán said:

"You were guided. She was going to stand there while she'd think out the whole story."

He picked up the spoon and followed her, jerking his head to us to come too. Alonso had disappeared as soon as Sarah had come out into the hallway. We filed into the kitchen after her. Here the heat was powerful, from a big stove set back in the wall in a recess. Some bright charcoal glowed through the bars in the front of it, and we could hear the pot of sauce bubbling fatly. Sarah had taken another spoon and she was stirring it vigorously. Now she took it off the stove and placed it on the huge white wooden table that filled the middle of the room. Out of the oven she took a big, round, brown dish already piled high with rice. Then she poured the sauce over it and mixed it well in. From another pot on the stove she took spoonfuls of mussels in their shells and laid them on top in a pattern like a wheel.

By the time she had finished this operation, the three of us were gathered in an eager, panting little crowd at her elbows. We watched the spoon go back and forth, licking our lips, which had suddenly become wet. A pain started in my jaws, from the way that I had clenched them.

Suddenly Sarah looked up from her concentrated work and said:

"Ye're hungry."

"Yes, ma'am," said Jim.

"Sit down," she said.

We pulled out three straw-seated chairs from the table and sat down. In a moment she was ladling her gorgeous mash into three deep plates and handing us spoons to eat it with.

In Connemara, no one would think of making a dish of rice and fish. We had never eaten such food before, but as it went down I thought that it was the most heavenly mixture in the whole world. We cleaned our plates and she filled them again, until there remained in us not a single nook or cranny, not a single small square inch that was not satisfied.

At last, one by one, we laid down our spoons. I yawned like a cat that would be full of milk, stretching his rounded stomach in the sun. Then I looked at the dish. It was nearly empty.

"We've eaten it all," I said, shocked at our bad manners. "We've left nothing for yourselves." This put an idea into my head. "What family have you?"

"My husband, of course," Sarah said. "And three boys. Two of them are out ploughing today, but Juan is here."

And there behind us, at the kitchen door, was the boy that had been at the quay when we arrived. He was dark-skinned and dark-haired, and his eyes were a deep shining brown, the color of bog water. I could not see the smallest resemblance between him and his mother.

"He's the image of his father," Sarah said, seeing us look from one of them to the other. "The two others are more like me."

She spoke in Spanish to the boy, and he came into the room and shook hands with each of us in turn.

"He knows plenty of English too," she said. "Later on, when you have had a sleep, he will show you the rest of the village."

Now I saw that we were all yawning like fish. Sarah said that we could sleep for an hour or two.

"Everyone sleeps after rice," she said. "It's the natural thing to do."

It felt fine and natural to us too. Just as we stood up, however, we heard steps in the hallway and then the rest of the family came in. Sarah looked at them in alarm.

"Tomás, why are you back? Are the horses all right?" she asked in English.

"Yes, yes. Juan came to the field and told us that there were visitors from Ireland, so we just finished the furrow and came home to welcome them."

Her husband was a tall man with shining, curly hair that fell all over his forehead. He looked us over with great interest.

"We don't have many visitors from Ireland in Commillas," he said.

"This boy is my cousin," Sarah said, taking Ciarán's arm, "and these are his friends. My father sent them."

"He sent them! Why didn't he come himself?"

"He's too old for that now," Sarah said. "It's twenty years."

"He would have come if we had given him any encouragement," I said. "But we thought the journey would be too hard for him. It was hard enough for us."

"He wants me to go back to the island," Sarah said softly. "He has the house all ready, the boys said, whitewashed and lovely."

"And do you want to go?"

"I'd like to see it again. Often I think of it, especially in the early morning when there would be a line of clouds above the sea, and the dew on the grass, and the birds singing, and a little wind blowing the scent of the flowers so that the air is full of it."

"We have all that here in Commillas, and more."

"We have, it's true. I don't know why it's not the same. The sea sounds different. You know that all around Ireland, guarding the shores, there are four great waves. I remember their names: the wave of Tóime; the wave of Ruairí—that's the one in the north; the wave of Clíona——" She stopped and looked distressed. "I can't remember the name of the fourth one! How could I have forgotten it?"

"Because you made your home here with me, in Commillas," Tomás said.

"That's not a good reason. Only a bad person can forget his own country."

"If you don't go back—if you don't meet your own people sometimes——"

"Perhaps one of the boys would remember." She turned to us and asked: "What is the name of the fourth wave?"

None of us could answer her. I knew it as well as I knew my own name but no amount of concentration would bring it to my tongue now.

"Look at that!" Sarah said. "They are only a few days away from home and already they're beginning to forget. Another month and they would be forgetting the name of the dog at home, and whether they have three cats or four in the house, and the date of the pattern. I must go back to see it all again, and to see my father."

"I'll go with you, of course," Tomás said. "You might need me."

"And I'll go too," said Juan. "All my life I'm hearing about Ireland."

We did not know what to say. The thought of bringing three people, one of them a woman, on our little *Santa Maria* was frightening. We had bargained only for Sarah, and we had decided to give her the cabin to herself on the return journey while we would sleep on the deck. Now I realized that even with Sarah alone this would be an impossibility. Even for us, conditions of living on the *Santa Maria* had been too primitive. I had guessed that old Colman's daughter would be tough and strong, and this she certainly seemed to be. Now we had to remember that she was still a woman. It had seemed like a wonderful idea that we should sail back to the very spot from which she had left, and hand her over to her father, but now it came to me all at once that this had been only a silly dream. And supposing we lost her on the way home! If one of those squalls were to come and if she were washed overboard! Or if we were drowned and she were left to sail the boat alone!

Disaster piled on disaster in my imagination until I could stand it no longer.

"We won't all fit on our little boat," I said.

Sarah's husband laughed at my alarmed expression.

"Of course not," he said. "We'll go on our own trawler. We can go in convoy so that one of us can help the other if we have to."

"You have your own trawler?" Jim said with respect.

"Of course. And it's the same one that I used to kidnap my wife the day long ago."

"So that's all settled," Sarah said. "In the evening we'll talk about when we'll go and a lot of other things as well. I want to hear about everything that has happened in Ireland since I went away."

She hustled us out of the room saying:

"Now you can sleep while I cook another pot of rice."

Juan brought us upstairs and showed us a huge, cool room with three beds, where he and his brothers slept. We rambled over to the beds like sleepwalkers, and lay down to sleep.

(8)

In the cool of the evening we woke up. The room was almost dark. Beyond the long windows, the trees were stirring gently in the breeze and we could hear voices of children playing in the square.

I stretched to my full length, feeling luxuriously the softness of the mattress under me. It was like paradise to lie in this quiet room after our voyage on the *Santa Maria*. My respect for Captain Hennessy had increased greatly since I had left home. I wondered how we would have endured three months of those spiky straw mattresses, and a diet of fish and hard bread and black tea. Then I remembered that the people who sail the Atlantic in small boats never sail them home again. They always have their boats hoisted onto big ships and they come home in comfort. This made me feel that perhaps I was not so unheroic after all.

Now I saw that Ciarán was awake too. His voice came quietly out of the dimness at the other side of the room:

"She's a fine woman indeed, is Sarah. She's all they said and more. And her husband is as good as any man she would have found in Connemara. A fine, upstanding man—not like that creeper you saw on the island."

"Do you know him?" I asked in surprise.

"I know him, but he doesn't know me," Ciarán said.

"Whenever I go to Inishownan, of course I visit the shop that my cousin has. It seems to me that Morgan MacDonagh is always there, sitting on a barrel looking down into a pint of black porter."

"Has he not got a place of his own to work in?"

"It's his mother's land. She's hale and hearty, as old as a field. No man can be working all the time, and when Morgan wants a rest he can't ever go home."

"Why not?"

"His old one do be after him all the time, they say, wanting him to find a nice girl with a bit of money in the bank and plenty of land. After Sarah went away, a few times he got friendly with girls, but his old one always thought they weren't good enough. They say he'll have to take a Yank in the latter end, some yellow old one burned up with the heat of New York and wrinkled with years of labor to make her stocking full of gold."

I thought all this was very sad, especially that Morgan MacDonagh could never rest by his own fireside but had to sit on a barrel in a shop, with his forlorn state obvious to all.

"Perhaps he was fond of Sarah long ago," I suggested.

Ciarán gave a kind of snort.

"They say he was fond of her the way a dog would be fond of his dinner." He stopped. "But sure, it was long before my time and it wouldn't be right for me to judge him. It could be, indeed, that he was as fond of Sarah as he was of Flaherty's Island."

"Old Colman didn't think there was anything wrong with his wanting the island."

"That's what he said, but all he really wanted was to have Sarah living at home with him always. If I know old Colman, himself and Morgan would have been at each other's throats in a week—the first time that Morgan would act like the owner of Flaherty's Island."

"I suppose they would." I could imagine the scene, with

Colman prancing around in a temper and his son-in-law driven to similar fury by the old man's insults. "Sarah had an escape, for sure," I said.

"From what I can hear, she was in no danger of making that mistake," Ciarán said. "Her father was the only one who believed they would be married. Her sister told her from the very first day that she should have nothing to do with Morgan MacDonagh. He wasn't even a good fortune hunter—his old one has all the spirit knocked out of him. Whatever girl would marry him would have to be like a mother to him as well as a wife."

We roused up Jim, who was still sleeping soundly. He glared at us and rolled himself deeper into the mattress but we spilled him out of that onto the floor. This kind of thing can't be done quietly. Before we had finished, Juan was in the room offering to show us the whole village before suppertime.

Every part of that village was beautiful. It had a marketplace with a big church at one side and a covered place for the people to stroll in, safe from the heat of the sun. It had narrow, hilly, cobbled streets with tall houses whose lower windows were barred inhospitably. We followed one street away uphill and came to a huge monastery from whose garden we looked out over the little bay. In the dusk I could just make out the shape of our *Santa Maria* moored to the quay. The sea was smooth, with patches of red from the evening sun. All around us the air was full of the scent of flowers.

On our way home we passed by the village cemetery and were astonished to see that the people were not buried under the ground at all but were put into niches in the high walls. We value our land very highly in Ireland, I thought, but we can always spare a few yards of ground for our dead friends and relations.

While he was showing us all these wonders, Juan was ask-

ing us about our country—was it true that it was always green
and that it was more beautiful than Spain, and that if you
went out late at night the Good People would catch you and
take you away with them and not let you come home for a
hundred years? It was all quite true, we told him solemnly,
especially the last part.

We found that his mother had told him all the old stories
that they tell in the chimney corner in Ireland on the long
winter evenings. He knew about the great hero Fionn Mac-
Cumhaill and Bran his dog, and his son Oisín whose mother
was a deer, and his great army of heroes, called the Fianna. It
was easy to see that in all her years away from Ireland, Sarah
had not, after all, forgotten much about it. I guessed that it
must have hurt her a great deal not to have been able to visit
her own country for so long.

Sarah was waiting for us when we got back to the house.
Dusk had fallen, but the children were still playing outside.
Indeed the square seemed to me like a huge common parlor,
with room for everyone. People had brought kitchen chairs
outside their houses, and the women sat there chatting to
each other and getting on with their knitting. In the middle
of the square there was a big open space between the trees,
and groups of boys and girls strolled up and down there. The
boys kept apart from the girls, which I thought a very strange
thing. They were beautiful girls, dark-haired and dark-
skinned, and they were dressed like flowers.

"We don't have supper until ten o'clock," Sarah said, "so
we can sit outside and make a few plans."

Seeing our dismayed looks, she opened a cupboard and
gave us a little, long-shaped loaf of bread each. To this day,
all my memories of Commillas are connected with the taste
of that wonderful bread. We helped Sarah to bring out chairs
and we sat there in the dimness, chewing comfortably and
talking about the voyage home.

"Did you never think of going someday on the trawler

without warning?" I asked Sarah after a while. "Did you never think of just walking into your father's kitchen, some-day, and saying: 'God save all here!' and sitting down to the fire as if you had never been away?"

"Oh, yes, I thought of that," Sarah said. "But I was afraid that my father would disrespect my husband and then I'd have to go away again and perhaps never be able to come back. You'll see it when you have your own wife," she added after a pause. "Until you're married, your parents are the first. After you're married, they're the second. That's how the world goes."

"Of course," I said, glad that she had not been offended by my question.

We told her about our voyage, how we had had fair weather until the squall had nearly overturned us and of our diet of fish. Her husband came and sat with us while we were describing it.

"You were lucky," he said. "That little boat of yours is too small to have come so far. The man that let three boys out in that boat must be soft in the head."

"He didn't let us. We didn't ask his leave," I said furiously. "And the *Santa Maria* is the finest boat that ever left Ross-more."

"Easy, easy on! You fly at me just as a Spaniard would. On the way home, I'll have a chance to see how she sails."

Then we had to tell the history of the *Santa Maria,* and I could see while we were talking that his respect for her in-creased. He questioned us closely about her dimensions and about the kind of timber that had been used.

"I know it's larch," I said, "but that's all I know. My grandfather got so cross in the end that he wouldn't let any-one know what he was doing."

"So he built just one good boat when he could have built thousands."

"He couldn't. He was too old."

"I mean that if he had explained what he was doing, every boat from now on would be so much the better of it."

My grandfather had never thought of this, of course. He had cared only for the *Santa Maria*.

We had supper at ten o'clock, all sitting around the kitchen table. The two older boys were very silent, perhaps because they knew no language but their own. They were fine, tall men with broad shoulders and broad, powerful hands. But for the language they spoke, they might have been Connemara men. I thought how old Colman would be proud of them, if he could have them on the island for a while, to show them off to his relations in Carraroe.

"Can the whole family come on the trawler?" Ciarán asked, perhaps thinking of the same thing.

"Only Juan," Sarah said. "Someone must stay to look after the horses and the cattle. If things go well, the others can go later."

Jim said:

"It would be well for them to go soon. The sight of them would be enough to keep Morgan MacDonagh off the island."

"Morgan MacDonagh! What brings him to Flaherty's Island?" Sarah asked sharply.

Ciarán said in his easy drawl:

"We don't know for certain sure what brings him there but we can guess. From what I hear, he always had his eye on it."

"He had, poor Morgan," Sarah said. "Did he never get a wife?"

"He's still waiting," said Ciarán. "Morgan is slow but sure. I'd say he'd be faithful, if he'd be as fond of his wife as he is of Flaherty's Island."

It astonished me to hear a boy talk like this, so cynically. Sarah did not like it either. She said:

"It was always easy to laugh at poor Morgan. Tomás, you

127

remember him—the slow-moving man that wanted to marry me long ago."

"The sad-looking man," Tomás said. "I remember him."

"The boys saw him on the island," Ciarán said. "He thought there was no one there. He had seen old Colman go off to Carraroe in the currach. He came up to the house and opened the door and went inside, and they found him standing in the middle of the kitchen."

"God bless my soul! Did you speak to him?"

"We didn't get a chance," Jim said. "He ran like a hare when he saw us, off to his currach and away home with him."

"But why did he come? Did he say no word at all? Did he—did he steal anything?"

"I think he has a mind to steal the whole island," Ciarán said. "All the way out here on the boat I've been going over and over what John and Jim told me, and that's what I believe now. I think that Morgan MacDonagh is hoping that old Colman will die soon, God between us and all harm. Then he would move into the house before anyone would have time to stop him, and there's very few that would want to fight to get him out of it again. If he had a bit of luck, the island and the house and everything in it would be left to him in a few years."

"Do you think it could happen like that?"

"It could, faith. Who is to prevent it? It would be no business of anyone on Inishownan except your sister Mary and I'm thinking she nor her family wouldn't do much."

"Why not?"

"Because as the world knows, your father said she was not to set foot on the island again as long as she lives," I said. "He told us about it himself, and he was fierce about it. He said he'd haunt her," I finished quickly in a low voice, almost afraid to say it at all.

Sarah was silent for a few minutes. Then she said in a heavy, sad tone, more to her husband than to the rest of us:

"Indeed it is time I went home to visit my father."

It was midnight when we went to bed again, weighed down with rice and tomatoes and shellfish, and a sweet sticky cake which we washed down with red wine. This combination is sure to give anyone a sound night's sleep. We woke to the sound of the village going about its business in the broad daylight of the next morning.

After breakfast we went down to the quay to have a look at the *Santa Maria,* and to clean her up for her voyage home. I remember well how my first sight of her that morning affected me. Until then she had seemed to me a good-sized boat, that you could be proud to own. At home I would cheerfully have filled her up with half a dozen young heifers and sailed her in to Galway from Rossmore, or I would have loaded her with turf four or five feet above the waterline and taken her over to the Aran Islands on a calm day.

Now suddenly she looked no bigger than a scallop shell. She looked so small that I wondered how three people could have sailed on her at all, not to mind coming all the way to Spain from Ireland. Part of the reason for this was that all around her there were trawlers and fishing boats moored. The smallest of them was three times the size of our *Santa Maria.* Another reason why she looked so forlorn was that she was incredibly dirty. It was hard to believe that she had taken to the water sprucely, for the first time, less than a month ago.

"We can give her a scrub, at least," I said.

Jim said:

"Doesn't she look like an old currach? How did we ever get her so dirty?"

"We should have scrubbed her down every day with soap and water," I said. "That must be why they're always scrubbing in the Navy, because if you give up for one day your ship is a disgrace."

The reason for it was, of course, that she had been our

kitchen and our bedroom and our living room for the length of our voyage. We had gutted our fish on her and raked out our ashes and shed our crumbs and our potato skins, only half clearing up each time we had finished a meal.

"We'll need buckets and scrubbing brushes and soap," Ciarán said. "Sarah will have all those things."

She had, and she lent us a sweeping brush as well and gave us some good advice. We went to work, first brushing over every part of her and then working the scrubbing brushes by turns. We found that she was caked with salt over her new blue paint. This washed off easily, and immediately she looked better. Juan got a pot of white paint and touched up the letters of her name. Gradually she began to be herself again.

While we worked, we had noticed an interested line of spectators gather on the quay above us. We could hear approving sounds, and then Juan translated some of the comments that were being made:

"An industrious boy is as rare as a rose in winter."

"Perhaps all Irish boys work as well as these do."

"No, no! I have seen them—these are exceptional boys."

When we knew what they were saying, of course, we redoubled our efforts, standing back now and then to admire the results. In this way we got to the end of our task, and it was only when it was finished that we realized all at once that our arms and legs were stinging with strange pains.

"How do women do these things?" Jim said in wonder. "The next time I see my mother scrubbing the kitchen table, I'll have a closer look at her way of doing it."

"Practice is what does it," Ciarán said. "They grow special muscles for it in time."

Before we had finished, Tomás came down to look over his trawler, which was moored to a buoy a little out from the quay wall. She was a trim, tight little ship, perhaps sixty feet long. We had noticed her long before Tomás arrived, be-

cause of her name, *Santa Maria,* being the same as ours. We went out with him on his dinghy and climbed aboard.

Everything about that trawler delighted me. She had a glass-fronted cabin to shelter the man at the tiller from the wind and the rain. She had an oil-powered engine that would take her over the seven seas of the world. She had complicated gear for casting her trawl, that would catch every fish and his grandmother in her path. She had a cabin where six men could sleep on bunks, like loaves of bread on shelves. She had a tiny galley with a chimney to take off the smoke, and different kinds of pots and pans.

All this magnificence impressed me very much and yet a strange thing was that I had no more wish to own her than I would have had to own the Taj Mahal. Perhaps it was because a hundred things about her told me that she was the wrong shape for our waters. She was too high in her hull to stand up to long hours of huge waves, as we have them, that keep rolling along one after the other without rest. There were many other things about her that seemed to me unsafe, but most of all I distrusted her engine. What would happen if it broke down, I wondered. She would be quite helpless then, whereas our *Santa Maria* would heave to like a bird, even without a mast. Later in my life I began to put some trust in machinery, but at that time I was all for the natural way of doing things.

"Tomás," I said suddenly, "how did you survive that terrible storm on the night you took Sarah away? Old Colman thought for a long time that you were both drowned."

"The thought did nothing to soften his heart," Tomás said grimly. "He wrote a terrible letter to Sarah, God forgive him. He said the storm was a sign of the anger of God, that she should have left her father as she did. You'd almost think he was sorry we weren't sunk by the same storm. In fact we only had a little of it. We got away from Ireland quickly, because of our engines. The old man forgot that—he thought we had spent the night fighting the sea and the wind. All we saw was an hour or two of a good hard blow and then we were out of it. If we had been depending on sail, I wouldn't be talking to you now."

It was strange to think that old Colman had suffered more hardship from his night on the cliff-top than Tomás and Sarah had done in the storm. If anything were a judgment of God, surely that was it.

While we had dinner, Sarah questioned us closely about the state of her father's health. As delicately as we could, we told her that he was in powerful condition for his age but that himself and his clothes both needed a washing.

"He does his own housekeeping, and his own washing and mending," I said. "He's good at the housekeeping."

"And his clothes?"

"He's not too bad-looking when he comes over to Carraroe," said Ciarán. "He always has a good jersey and Mrs. MacDonagh in the shop sells him the odd pair of trousers. At home he wears his old clothes to spare the new ones. The wind do be whistling through the holes in them, but he doesn't seem to bother."

It occurred to me that it would be a very good thing if old Colman were to gallop home and change into his better clothes before Sarah would see him. This would have to be left to chance, however, as we would have no hope of landing before the trawler would. Perhaps Sarah knew what to expect. As she prepared for the journey, she took a blue suit of her husband's from a big press in the hall.

"This would fit my father, I think," she said to us. "When I saw him last he was about the same size as Tomás."

"He hasn't grown since then," Ciarán said. "It will fit him fine."

We were to start off the next morning, with a promise of good weather until the equinox. That time of the year always brought the worst storms, and I hoped we would be safe on dry land in time to escape them. Tomás had said he would give us a tow from time to time, so that we knew the voyage home would be shorter. Ciarán was not so pleased about this.

"Won't we be at home all our lives?" he said. "We won't get a chance to sail to Spain every year, you may be sure."

But Jim and I had both got a sudden longing to see our parents again and to tell them about our adventure. We felt that it would be wrong to prolong our absence from them by as much as a day. Ciarán understood this and agreed with us, but something about him suggested to me that he was often pleased to be a lone bird with no one to account to except his grandmother.

Our sleep was sweet again that night, and we savored the softness of our beds, remembering the bags of straw. Juan wakened us at the dawn and took us out to see the farm. It was fine smooth land without a rock or a stone to be seen. What amazed me was to see a two-story house for the cattle alone—the stable part downstairs and the feed above. The cattle were small and black, rather like our Kerry cows. There were twenty-four of them, Juan said. He showed us the pigs too—great, hulking, black-and-white ones with flopping ears. They looked so different from ours that I felt quite bewildered. Until then I had thought that all pigs were alike the world over. It was almost a comfort to observe that they smelled the same.

After I had seen the farm, I knew finally how unjust old Colman had been to Tomás.

"We must get him here to see all this," I said to Ciarán. "Then he'll stop talking about foreign fly-by-nights. Tomás could buy Flaherty's Island and everything on it if he wanted to."

"He should come, surely," Ciarán said, and we could see that he was impressed too. "It's the only thing that will stop him from giving out about foreigners."

Back at the house we found Sarah ready to leave. Bags of

provisions had already gone on board the trawler and she was busy giving last-minute instructions to the two boys who were staying at home. They were to go to a neighbor woman every day to eat, and they were to eat plenty so that they would be nice and fat when she would come back. Juan translated this for us and he added:

"She needn't fear for them. They'll eat that neighbor out of house and home."

"How is it that you know English so well and they don't know a word?" I asked in astonishment.

"They're lazy about it," Juan said. "They never wanted to learn. But I always did. I always wanted to know all about Ireland. I know some Irish too, and a few songs that my mother sings. There's another reason, maybe. When my brothers were small, my mother was angry with her father and she never talked much about Ireland. But by the time I came along, perhaps she was beginning to change her mind. She told me stories and sang me songs when I was small, that she never did for the older ones. Perhaps she was getting lonely. I've wanted to see Ireland for a long time, and I want to see my grandfather."

"I hope the old rasper will be civil to him when he sees him," said Jim into my ear as Juan went aboard the dinghy with his parents.

There was a crew of two on the trawler, as well as Tomás and Juan, but it was decided that they would not be needed on this journey as Jim was very anxious to find out how to sail her. It seemed to us that the whole population of the village had come down to see us off. There were women and children there too, and as I listened to their comments I guessed that they were probably saying exactly the same things as our own people had said when we went away from Rossmore:

"With the help of God they'll go safely. It's a very small boat."

"But the weather is good and they're good sailors."

"So long as they don't do anything foolish. The best of us can be foolish at times."

Then, as we cast off:

"Good luck!"

"God speed you!"

"God protect you!"

"Come back soon!"

By the tone of voice I guessed that they were saying these things and I determined there and then to learn their language. We waved and called out to the people in Irish:

"Good-by! We'll be back again next year!"

Then we sailed across the harbor and took a towrope from the trawler. Tomás said:

"As long as the weather is good, we'll tow you. If it gets up a storm, you might do better on your own, but I've often towed a Connemara hooker into harbor when the weather was bad."

It was a tame way to sail home, perhaps, but it certainly was much faster and we were glad to be free of the responsibility of finding our course. Jim was a much better sailor than I was and he and Ciarán spent long hours on the trawler, learning from Tomás how to use the compass and the chart.

When they went onto the trawler, Juan came aboard the hooker with me. While I was alone with him, I had my first lessons in Spanish. I did not find it a difficult language, and even a little knowledge of it had the effect of making me feel sure that I would go back to Spain someday.

For the whole of that journey we had calm, sunny weather. Even in the treacherous part where we had seen the squall dancing along, this time it was as flat as a pan of milk. We soaked in the sun, turning more brown with every day that passed. When we approached the Irish coast, we thought that it must surely change but it did not. It almost seemed as if

September were paying back August for the vicious storm that had wrecked the *Santa Maria*.

Flaherty's Island looked like a paradise when we saw it in the distance, pale blue and shimmering in the sun. Beyond it the Aran Islands were a darker blue.

It was noon when we saw the island first. All afternoon long, I could see Sarah standing at the bows of the trawler gazing toward her old home. I thought what a miracle it would be if her father happened to be on the cliff-top today, and could watch our approach, but as we came nearer we saw that he was not there.

We had told Tomás to sail around the island to the little harbor, as old Colman had instructed us. Presently he cut down his speed and cruised along slowly, watching for the way in. Ciarán was with him in the wheelhouse, piloting him. Still there was no sign of life. A dreadful gloom overcame me. This was the moment of our greatest triumph and still I was oppressed with the feeling that some disaster had happened in our absence.

I had the sense to be quiet. There was nothing to be done until we had safely moved into the harbor and were moored to the rock that served as a quay.

(9)

We lay right behind the trawler. We took nothing from either boat, but stood on the quay in a group, listening. It was very quiet. The sea slapped against the smooth rocks. Sea gulls called high above us, and far out on a reef I could hear some small bird give a mournful repeated whistle. It was almost seven o'clock and the light was beginning to go. Over us, a transparent, greenish sky was decorated with a feathery moon and one star. I felt suddenly very cold.

Tomás took Sarah's arm and said gently:

"Now you can lead us. Do you remember the way?"

"I remember it," she said.

Led by Tomás and Sarah, we started up the path to the grass-grown road. Sarah's back was straight and she walked quite firmly, but I guessed that she was cruelly disappointed at the deserted feel of the island. Yet she cannot have expected anything else. It would be better when we would get nearer to the house, I thought.

The cultivated fields looked more alive. A last beam of sunlight lit up the barley so that it looked like dark gold. As we approached the house, however, the same depression took hold of me again. I would have given anything in the world for Sarah's first sight of the house to have been cheerful. The door should have been standing open, showing the glow of a blazing fire. The lamp might even have been lit, and we might have seen old Colman springing around the kitchen as he prepared his supper.

The door was shut. Not a light showed anywhere. It had the motionless feel of an empty house, a house where life had been suspended for a while so that it need not even bother to breathe. We knocked, but I knew Colman was not there.

Ciarán turned the handle and pushed the door inward. We crowded together, peering into the dimness. By the cold air, I knew that the fire had gone out. Still I said:

"He must have gone over to Carraroe."

Ciarán went across and felt the ashes in the hearth.

"Cold," he said. "This fire has been out for days. If he were gone to Carraroe, the seed of the fire would be buried in the ashes, waiting for him to build it up when he'd come back."

"Perhaps he's staying with your grandmother," Jim said.

"If he is, it's the first time in history," said Ciarán. "They have a joke about him in Carraroe, that he never sleeps anywhere but at home. Even if the weather is bad, he always gets here somehow."

"Then where is he?" Sarah said sharply. "Was he well when you left him?"

"Hale and hearty, better than ourselves," Ciarán said. "We told you that, and it was the truth."

He took the oil lamp down from its hook on the wall and lit it. At once the kitchen seemed to come to life. We brought turf from the little pile against the wall and got the fire going. Gently Ciarán took Sarah's shawl and hung it on the hook behind the door. Then he made her sit on the hob close to the fire.

"Now we'll get water and make tea," he said.

He took the water can that stood on a bench by the back door and went outside. A moment later I slipped out after him.

He was waiting for me at the gable of the house. There was
no need for any discussion.

"Find the goats," he said. "See if they have been milked.
I'm going to look around a bit too."

I set off at a run up the hill. Dusk had fallen and the walls
and the spiky thorn-bushes that grew here and there in the
fields were jet black. The sky had darkened over, except for
a green strip above the sea. The thin moon gave only a dim

light, but after a while I found the patch of moving shadow where the goats were. They were quiet, nibbling softly at the dewy grass. I went among them and touched their milk bags one by one. They were all empty. I looked around for kids, that might have milked their mothers dry, but there were none.

A terrible suspicion flashed into my mind. I put it away with all my strength. I ran down the hill so fast that an out-cropping rock nearly sent me into the next world. Ciarán was coming back with the full can of water from the well.

"I found them," I said, panting for breath. "They're milked. Someone milked them."

"Quiet! The eggs are gone too. I thought I'd find the hens all sitting on clutches of them, thinking the good times had come. Someone has been taking them."

"Old Colman?"

"Someone else."

"Morgan MacDonagh?"

"Maybe. But where is Colman? How will we face Sarah with our story?"

We decided to say nothing just then. Back in the kitchen, the blazing fire had made everyone more cheerful. We put on the kettle and made some tea, using the good china cups from the dresser as we knew Colman would have done if he had been at home. I opened the bread cupboard, expecting to find it empty, but there was a fresh soda-loaf inside. I took it out and cut slices for everyone.

"Look at that," Sarah said. "A house with fresh bread in it is not long empty."

I did not mention what I had noticed, that the loaf was bigger than could have been made in old Colman's pot-oven. The thoughts that followed on this observation were so black that I could not bear them alone.

"I'll go down to the boat for some bedding," I said. "If

we're all to sleep in the house tonight, we'll need to bring up our gear."

"I'll come with you and bring ours," Juan said instantly.

"And I'll come to carry things," Ciarán said in his slow drawl.

Jim reached for the lantern that hung on a nail by the door but he did not light its candle end.

"Come along then," he said.

We were gone before the older people could say a word. Since they were not familiar with the house and with the old man's habits, I hoped that they were not yet suspicious as we were.

We would have preferred if Juan had stayed with his parents but there was no time to waste in thinking of excuses for sending him back. As soon as we were well away from the house, we stopped. Ciarán said:

"We'll divide the island between us. If we don't find him——"

Juan said at once:

"You think he's somewhere on the island! I thought you said that no one else lives here."

"That's right."

"Then where could he be?" Juan insisted.

"We don't know," Ciarán said desperately. "We left him safe and counting the days until we'd be back. We only know that it's a queer thing he's not here to welcome us."

"Perhaps he saw us coming and hid himself?" Juan suggested. "Perhaps he was afraid to meet my mother after so long, and my father. Perhaps he was shy."

"Shy! That's one thing he never was in his life," Ciarán said with a snort. Then he added hurriedly: "Of course it could be so. It could be, indeed. We'll have to find him anyway. You come with me and we'll search. John and Jim can go together."

He caught my shoulder and turned me away from the others, so that he could say softly:

"I'm going to try the caves and the base of the cliffs to the west. You can search the eastern half of the island. Go through every field. Look for signs of——"

Before I could question him more, he had seized Juan and said:

"Come along. Quickly. We'll meet here in half an hour."

Then he was gone, leaving me with a feeling that there was something cold and wet sitting on my neck.

Jim said:

"Where will we begin?"

"Here. It will save time."

Soft light from the moon gave everything a gray color. We could not see very far, but little feet that scuttered away as we approached told us that we could be seen. We worked through the fields at either side of the road, aware that our task was impossible but afraid not to carry out Ciarán's instructions. I began to see dark shapes that melted away when we came near them. I began to hear sounds of breathing, as if we were surrounded by an army. The walls at either side of the little grassy road seemed to have grown taller. Whenever we climbed over them, brambles grabbed at our bare ankles and nettles leaned forward to sting us.

The ruined houses were the hardest to enter. It seemed to me that there was a ghost in every one of them, the sad spirit of the man who had built the house and whose descendants had all gone away to foreign countries. I wished the thought had not come to me as we searched the roofless houses one by one. It was an easy search since there were only three tiny rooms in each house. But I could feel the time slipping away and still we had no sign of the old man. I did not dare to think of what we might find.

When we did find him, I wondered why we had not thought to look there first of all. I had noticed the old school on our first day on the island, when Colman had gone across to Carraroe in the currach with news that we were safe. Then it had seemed a strange thing that among all those ruined buildings, two should have slated roofs—the school and the teacher's house beside it. Some of the slates had been blown off by storms but a good many of them were in position. The school building stood toward the back of a little walled yard which may once have been paved with stones. I remembered that the grass had grown very short and thin there. Two broken stone pillars stood at either side of its entrance, where once there had been a gate.

We came on the school by a side road that ran along by its gable. This was a high blank wall of stone, rather near the road, on which it cast a huge shadow. The wind seemed colder there.

"If he's alive, this is where we'll find him," I said.

"You're right, of course," Jim said softly. "Ciarán thought of the cave."

"No one could live long in the cave. Do you remember the cold of it?"

"I do, well. 'Twas like a grave. How many days would you say he's gone from the house?"

"Three or four. The hearth was stone cold."

We came slowly into the schoolyard. Bits of broken slates hidden in the grass pricked our feet cruelly. I could not remember the door of the building, whether it had been sound or rotten. When we reached it, we saw that it was the original door of the school but it was in fairly good condition. We had a similar school in Rossmore, a one-roomed building with a little porch to serve as a cloakroom stuck on the front of it. In every part of Connemara where I had been, they were the same.

A strange thing about this school was that though it was so long out of use it still had the smell of school. It came to us at the very door. There is no other smell like it—a mixture of pencil parings and ink and turf smoke. I suppose it takes years to work up to a good school smell. In the fine new schools that are being built now, it will be a long time before the true flavor is reached.

The door was locked, of course. We moved the latch up and down and pushed with all our weight. It yielded a very little.

"A battering-ram is what we need," Jim said, "but we'll have to do our own battering."

He put down the lantern and we walked back about twenty paces from the door. Then we clasped our hands together to make sure that we would both hit the door at the same moment. I counted:

"One, two, three!"

And we began to run, shoulder to shoulder. A yard from the door I yelled:

"Now!"

We threw ourselves on the door with all our force, getting it with our shoulders. I thought mine was broken. It was a month before that night's bruise was gone.

The door flew open. We fell in a heap together on the floor of the porch. It was a wood floor, softly rotted here and there. We lay for a moment, stupefied. The we crawled to our feet, and I heard Jim rattling with matches as he lit the lantern. The little flame showed a second door. We saw at once that this had no lock but a latch only. We opened it and stood peering into the big, dark schoolroom.

Jim held the lantern high. We moved cautiously forward. Through the broken slates and the open, roofless patches above us, the night sky showed. A gray light came through the windows too. These had been barred across with wood, perhaps to keep hens from raising secret clutches of chickens inside.

It was a perfect prison, but poor old Colman, when we found him, would not have been able to escape. He was lying

against the wall by the fireplace, under the part of the roof that was best. He looked up at us almost sleepily. His hands were behind his back and I felt a black rage flow over me like a wave when I saw that they were tied with a piece of thick rope. We stood him on his feet and held him between us while I cut him free. He stretched his arms, very slowly, and said in a croaking voice:

"Ye weren't long in coming. Did ye see Sarah?"

"Yes, we brought her with us. She's above at the house, waiting to see you."

A look of astonishment and delight came over his face. We asked him no questions then, though we were like to die of curiosity about what had happened to him and who had imprisoned him. We took him by an arm each and helped him to walk out of the school into the yard. As we passed by the broken door he fetched it a kick, and from that moment onwards, gradually his strength seemed to return to him. I was surprised at this until I remembered the agility he had always shown in climbing the cliff path and rowing his currach and lifting great pots of feed for his pigs on and off the fire. Still, we could go only very slowly. Now that we had found him, we wanted to be quite sure that we would hand him over to Sarah in good condition. This was why we never let go our hold of him until we walked him into his own kitchen.

The moment that we looked into the kitchen we knew that Sarah and Tomás had become very agitated at our long absence. They were standing together at the fireplace. Tomás had his arm around her shoulders and he was saying something to her in Spanish. When they heard us, they turned. Then Sarah took a step forward and said uncertainly:

"My father?"

"Safe and sound," I said, "but he's cold as a stone."

She ran then. We waited for no more. Though this was the end of our mission, somehow we did not want to stay and watch their meeting. We had a good excuse to go—to find Ciarán and Juan and tell them that we had discovered Colman and brought him home.

We went toward the cliff, and met them coming along, slowly and dejectedly. When we had told our news, Ciarán said:

"I feared something much worse. Did you ask him any questions?"

"We thought he needed all his breath for walking," I said.

Burning with curiosity, still we gave Sarah and her father a few more minutes to make up for their twenty years' separation. Then we could stand it no longer. We ran back to the house and crowded into the kitchen together, all four of us panting like eager dogs.

Colman was sitting on the hob with his shins glowing in the light of the fire. He had a full glass in his hand, and he sipped it contentedly from time to time. He never took his eyes off his daughter, unless it was to glance briefly at her husband or her son. We got creepie stools from the corner and pulled them close to the fire. Colman was saying:

"Thursday or Friday, I don't remember now which day it was. Anyway, in the dark of the evening, I was here making my *brochán*, fine and independent, when I heard the step outside. It could be a cow, if I had a cow, I was thinking. But I haven't a cow, nor hadn't for years. It could be a donkey. It was too light to be a horse. That way my mind was running along and I hardly thinking of it at all, when who should come in at the door but Morgan MacDonagh.

"I didn't know him from a crow, of course. I hadn't laid an eye on Morgan since the day twenty-one years ago when he came over in the currach to ask if he could come courting Sarah. He was a quiet young fellow then, twenty-seven or twenty-eight years old. Very civil and quiet. They used to say the mother treated him like a boy, but faith he talked like a man, I thought——"

"Don't mind that old story," said Ciarán. "Go on with what happened."

"Yes, he came in and he stopped inside the door and he looked me all over. I wasn't in my Sunday best, I'll admit. I was in the clothes I'm wearing now, indeed. I meant to be all shined up for Sarah when she'd come but sure I never got the chance after all. That was his fault too."

Colman seemed to have most of his old energy back, at least so far as one could judge from the sharpness of his voice. He coughed a good deal and complained of a pain in his chest but otherwise it seemed that the fire and his glass of poiteen had revived him very well. Ciarán said:

"He looked you all over."

No one else said a word.

"He did so," said the old man, "up and down, mighty impertinent, the way you'd look over a cow at the fair."

" 'You're not too good, old man,' says he. 'You're no great shakes yourself,' said I. 'Can't you say God save all here, like a Christian, and come in and sit down?' He came in one step farther, and he said: 'Do you know me?' 'Never laid an eye on you before,' said I, 'but you're welcome anyway, and if you'll sit down I'll give you a sup of my *brochán.*' Still he didn't sit down. 'You did lay an eye on me,' he said. 'One time you were saying you'd be glad I'd marry your daughter.' 'Faith and I'm glad now that you didn't,' said I, 'for I'd like her to have a mannerly husband. You must be Morgan Mac-Donagh.' 'That's who I am,' said he.

"He came over to the fire then, and his two hands hanging from him. He wouldn't sit down, which I thought was a queer thing. I couldn't make out what brought him. If it was friendliness, why didn't he come twenty years ago?"

We could see that Sarah was in agonies to know what had happened. We knew it was no use trying to hurry Colman when he started telling a long story. Perhaps she knew it too, remembering it from her own youth.

"I said to myself, 'twasn't love that brought his here this time, whatever it was. Still, I wasn't sure, for a while.

"He said he wasn't getting younger, which was something I knew myself. He said it would be good for me to have someone around the place that would do a hand's turn for me now and then. He had a bit of *plámás* about how well I keep the place but he said that around about now my hands would be getting shaky and my feet would be getting slippery until someday I'd fall over my own toes and be killed."

This last part was said with savage derision.

"I thought he was a bit soft in the head," Colman went on. "He has a soft look about him at times. He had an idea, he said, that he would be the person that would help me in my old age. I was to make over the island to him, he said, and in return for that he would kindly allow me to live in my own house until I die. He'd do the farming for me and he'd feed the pigs, and he'd get a few young cattle to be eating the grass that's going to waste now. That way he'd make a bit of money so that he'd be able to entice a wife over to live with him and do the cooking.

"I was joking him for a while, telling him that most women don't give a curse for money or cows, but then I saw he was dead in earnest. He began to get cross and he said an old fellow like me had no business owning a whole island when there was them that were young and strong and in the need of land. ' 'Tis true for you,' said I, 'but that's the way the world goes: there isn't high nor low that doesn't be sometimes up and sometimes down.'

"With that, man, didn't he leap on me. Knocked me down on my own hearthstone, he did, and gripped my wrists and he glaring at me with red eyes like an old devil. I lay quiet. I knew I couldn't fight him. First I thought he was drunk and then I thought he was mad. But mad northwest he is, if he's mad at all. He held me there, and he bared his big greeny-yellow teeth at me and he said: 'Old man, you'll make over the island to me or it will be the worse for you.' 'It could hardly be worse for me,' says I, 'and I on the flat of my back and a big *amadán* threatening to grab my property.' A queer light came in his eye then and he said: 'It could be worse for you, indeed, and when it is, maybe you'll come to your senses.' 'I'm in my senses this minute,' said I, 'but I know them that aren't.'

"Well, to cut a long story short, didn't he tie my hands behind me the way they used to do to the prisoners in the bad old times, and he brought me down to the school and he left me there locked up. Once a day he'd bring me a bite to eat— bread he brought from Inishownan, and an egg or two, and a drop of milk. It was cold down there, I'm telling you. The only thing that kept me warm was the thought that ye were all coming back to me soon. Then in the nighttime I'd be thinking that the *Santa Maria* was a very small boat and Spain was a queer long ways away. If he had had the wit to come at night, between two and four in the morning, I'd have signed his paper for him like a shot. But he never came till the afternoon was well on and I used to have my courage back by that time."

"A paper? What paper?" Ciarán asked.

"A piece of an old copybook it was, by the looks of it. It was written on as neat as a tax collector would do it, that I Colman Flaherty hereby made over all my rights to Flaherty's Island here and hereafter to Morgan MacDonagh. Sarah," he said solemnly, "I'm fine and glad you didn't marry that man long ago.

"He didn't tie my feet, I'll say that for him, and sometimes he left my hands free. He knew I couldn't get out of that place because I hadn't the strength in me to break down the door. I was plotting, I needn't tell you, to cut the boards out of the windows with a piece of an old slate. But then I said to myself that it would be a waste of time because I wouldn't be able to leave the island nor get a bite to eat."

"You could have signed the paper," Tomás suggested. "Then when we would come along, you could change your mind."

"You're an innocent, good, decent man, as I can see," Colman said pityingly. "That paper said I was to be free to live on my island to the day of my death. How long do you think that day would be in coming, after I'd have signed the paper?" He stuck out his chin at each of us in turn. He had five days' growth of ragged hair on it. We were all silent. "A couple of days—that's how long I'd live!"

"God bless my soul!" said Sarah. "I'd hardly believe it. He wouldn't have the courage."

"He had been working up his courage for twenty years," Colman said. " 'Tis true, he has the heart of a mouse, but a mouse can bite if you drive him to it. I saw it in his eye, what he was planning."

"That old mother of his is the cause of it all," Ciarán said.

152

" 'Tis true, but the blame is his own for what he did," said Colman. "Mothers can't be blamed for everything."

It was clear that we had heard the whole story. No doubt Colman would be adding details to it for a long time but there was no need to wait for that. I said:

"The goats are milked and the eggs are gone. What time in the afternoon used he to come to the island?"

"Always before dark he used to come to me," Colman said. "I don't know what he did after that, or before it either. For all I knew, he could be living in my house. For all I know now, he could have sold all my pigs and made soup of my hens."

"No," Ciarán said. "The pigs are there, and the hens too. You were eating their eggs. It looks like he's gone home for the evening now, so we won't see him until tomorrow."

"Then we may as well bring up the bedding from the boats," Tomás said. "Sarah, you can stay here with your father. You can be chatting and filling his glass. We won't be long."

This time we took no lanterns. There were good ones on the trawler, Tomás said, and we could take one of those back with us if we needed it. There was enough light in the sky to show us our way and the less we had to carry besides the bedding, the better.

The road was narrow at the best of times and it was narrowed still further by the brambles and tall ferns that grew on either side. My senses must have been extra sharp that night, for I remember well the acid smell of the withering ferns and the way that they tickled my bare shins as I walked between them. We went in single file, myself in front, followed by Tomás and then Ciarán and Juan. Jim came last. We did not talk. The ugly taste of Colman's ordeal was still on us all. The night seemed full of strange sounds which became harmless when I analyzed them—the waves on the shore, the moan of the wind, the eerie whistle of a hunting owl. My skin prickled with alertness and I seemed to have put out antennae like a beetle, to feel what I could not see.

This was probably why I heard the creak of oars when it was inaudible to everyone else. A moment afterwards I doubted if I had heard it at all. Still I stopped and said in a whisper:

"Tomás! A boat coming!"

No one answered but they all stopped and stretched their ears for the sound. Ciarán said:

"I can't hear it."

"Neither can I, now," I said. "Perhaps it was imagination—now! Small stones, rolling!"

"God bless your ears," said Jim. "I can't hear a sound."

"Quiet!" said Tomás. After a moment he said: "There is something in the air, a sound, or a movement—I don't know which. Do you know where the nearest beach is?"

"This way."

Already Ciarán was on his way, running along the road, not too fast, so as to make less sound. The road we were on led straight to the natural pier where the two *Santa Marias* were moored. We followed Ciarán along a side road, no more than a track, that led to the beach. We slowed up as we came near it, and moved out quietly onto the grassy strip at the head of the beach. Below us there were several yards of rounded white stones the size and shape of ostrich eggs, perfectly formed by the eternal rolling of the high tides. There would be no question of walking quietly on them. Because of their shape, they moved incessantly under the feet with a sound like thunder. This was why we paused above them to see what was happening on the fine sandy stretch between the round stones and the sea.

A currach was there, we saw at once. A lone man was with it, quietly hauling it above the high-water line. It takes at least two men to carry a currach so there was no question of his lifting it. He was being extremely careful in pulling it over the sand, of course, because a hidden stone would have ripped a hole in it. We watched him for perhaps twenty seconds. There was no need for anyone to speak. We all understood what was to be done. Now was the moment for it, while he was busy.

Suddenly we were flying down over the rattling stones. For all their smooth appearance, they had a wicked trick of catching the toes between them. We fell, and got up and plunged onwards. The man stood, too startled to run. We fell on him, all together, and rolled him on the sand. We pinned his arms and legs and turned him on his back. Ciarán bent over him. Then he gave a short laugh.

"Good evening, Morgan," he said. The man said not a word. Probably he had no wind to say it with. Ciarán said: "It's Morgan MacDonagh, all right. Take a look at him, boys. Is he the one you saw in Colman's kitchen?"

We peered at him but the light was too dim to see by. I knew I would recognize him in a stronger light, by the bitter line of his mouth and by his thin soul, which had showed clearly but was so hard to describe.

We jerked him to his feet. Tomás said in a kindly tone:

"Breathe deeply several times. It will make you feel better."

I guessed that like myself he had begun to feel pity for Morgan—he looked so helpless and his story was so miserable. But it struck me then, as it often did later in my life, that it was a strange thing for a man who had suffered oppression himself to have treated someone else as badly. One would have thought he would have learned from his own sad life to be charitable and generous in his dealings. With him as with many another it seemed to have worked the other way: he had become sour, and jealous of the good fortune of everyone else.

Jim and Ciarán lifted the currach between them and laid it

down higher up the beach. Though he made no attempt to wriggle free, we held Morgan tightly. As we began to leave the beach, he spoke his first words:

"Where are you taking me?"

"To Colman Flaherty's house," said Ciarán. "He's above there, waiting for you."

Morgan gave a kind of low snarl, like a dog that was defending himself from several others. He had seemed so submissive that I was astonished. He spoke pantingly, drawing a painful breath between every few words:

"I suppose he has a long rigmarole about what I did to him. He's daft. He's too long in the world. He's gone soft in the head. He tells lies and stories. He asked me to come over here and help him out with the land—he had the wit to know he was getting old, at least. I came over, nice and neighborly. The next thing is that he's telling me I want to steal his land from him. I suppose he told you that. I suppose he told you I wanted him to sign it all away—that I said I'd make him do it. Old people do get queer. There's no trust in them. You come to help them and first of all they're glad. Then they get fidgety. Then they get suspicious. Then they say you're wishing them dead. Then they say you're planning their death. I suppose he told you that too."

"He told us that, all right," Tomás said.

Morgan said:

"He did, of course. He's clever enough to make you believe it too, of course."

Tomás said quietly:

"He'd have to be very clever to tie his own hands behind his back and lock himself into the schoolhouse where the boys found him nearly dead of the cold. Whoever wished for his death may have his wish yet. Colman is an old man—too old for such adventures."

Morgan turned his head to look directly at Tomás.

"You're a foreigner," he said, "for all your good English. Who are you?"

"I am Colman's son-in-law, Sarah's husband."

After that, Morgan made no more protests. We took turns at holding him, one at either side, while the other three kept close by. In this way we marched him up the hill to Colman's house.

(10)

A yard from the house door Morgan stopped and seemed to cling to the ground with his feet like an obstinate cow.

"I won't go in there," he said.

We heaved him onwards so that we almost flung him into the kitchen. Sarah and Colman sprang to their feet. Colman backed away to the far wall. His face took on a look of utter terror.

"Don't let him near me—don't let him touch me——" he said sharply, over and over.

Tomás said:

"Have sense, man! How can he touch you? He's all alone and there are seven of us. Sit down and be quiet."

Jim and I were afraid to look at each other lest we might burst into chuckles at this. Colman gave one startled look at Tomás and then he edged back into his place on the hob and sat down again. I wished long life to Tomás, if he could come around sometimes and give a few orders to Colman.

Morgan had his head down, but of course I recognized him clearly now as the man that we had surprised in the kitchen in Colman's absence. As I watched him, he lifted his head slowly and looked from one of us to the other, not with hatred nor anger but with a queer kind of resignation.

I could see now what Colman had meant when he had said

that Morgan had a soft look about him. He looked frightened, as well he might. For all he knew, we were the kind of people who would think it only right to serve him as he had served Colman, or perhaps worse. Still I got an impression that something else troubled him much more than his fear of us. I began to get curious about his mother and to wonder what kind of woman she could be. Even Colman had not been able to keep his family at home, and he was the toughest fellow I had ever met. I could not imagine how any woman could be more determined. The same thought must have been running in Tomás' mind for he said:

"You have a good piece of land in Inishownan, I've been told. Why then do you need to rob your neighbors?"

"There is land and money there," said Morgan, "but it's not mine. A man with no land is better dead."

This last was said with great bitterness. Tomás asked, as if the answer would be news to him:

"Who is the owner of the land, then?"

"My mother."

"You're as good a man as your mother any day. Why did you not force her to give you the land, as you tried to force Colman?"

We all moved closer to hear the answer to this question. In all my life I had never heard such straight talk. We don't have the habit of it in Connemara—we take the easy, roundabout way whenever we can, perhaps from politeness, perhaps to avoid trouble.

Morgan made no answer. Then Sarah spoke. She had said nothing until now but she had been watching her old admirer with a mixture of pity and impatient anger since he had been thrust into the house. Now she said softly:

"Why don't you say what you're thinking, Morgan? It would ease your heart." Still he made no answer. Sarah asked: "Are you afraid of her?"

"Yes, I am," he said, and his voice actually shook.

"How can you be?" Sarah said. "She's an old woman. She's weaker than my father."

"Yes, but your father is a good man."

This seemed to us all a very strange reply. We understood a moment later, however, when he added:

"My mother is a witch."

"God bless my soul," said Tomás. "What nonsense is this?"

"It's not nonsense at all," Morgan said sullenly. "She's forever over the fire boiling her little pots and saying queer rhymes and recitations. She told me she has put a curse on every one of her fields if I marry without her leave. 'Twas she that sent the red-haired woman."

"What red-haired woman?"

"The ghost of a red-haired woman, sailing alone in a hooker."

"A red-haired woman sailing?" I darted forward from the corner by the dresser to which Jim and I, feeling that we were overhearing a family affair that did not concern us, had retreated. "When? When did you see her?"

I shook his arm. He cowered away from me so that I had to let him go.

"Twice," he whined. "This morning and this afternoon, when I was coming here to milk the goats. But it's a ghostly woman sent by my mother——"

"Never mind your mother. Where was the hooker? What was the woman doing?"

"I kept well away from her. I wouldn't have gone near her for all the gold in the world."

"What was she doing?"

"Sailing the hooker, I told you. Sitting back in it with her chin up and her hair blowing in the wind." His voice dropped to a whisper, full of horror. "Red hair, blowing in the wind. I know my mother sent her. No woman ever had hair that color—'twas like a cockscomb. And sailing alone, what a man couldn't do."

"How could your mother send her?" Ciarán asked reasonably.

"With her spells, and with her curses. She has wind of what I'm planning, from her segoshioners that fly down the chimney to her when she's singing her rhymes. She told me that—those cronies of hers tell her everything. She can send one of them on a message from time to time. She sent this one as a warning to me that she knows what I'm planning—to leave Inishownnan altogether, and herself and her land and her moneybags, and come over here and make a decent living for myself."

"Decent!" said Sarah, and she gave a little laugh.

"She knows it," said Morgan, taking no notice of the interruption. "She'll have no one to plough the fields now and no one to thresh the corn. She'll have no one to wash the sheep and shear them, and bring the wool to the weaver. She'll have no one to take the young cattle in to the fair in Galway and pay the money into the Munster and Leinster Bank for her——"

"Did you pay the money into the bank for her too?" Tomás asked.

"Always. She'd have it counted, she'd tell me. Once only, I kept a few pounds but she knew it when I got home——"

"She was probably guessing," Sarah said briskly. "She couldn't know those things. She's only an old woman playing silly tricks."

Morgan rounded on her furiously.

"She's a witch, I'm telling you! She'll be sitting up on the hob when I go home, in the dark, with no light but the fire that boils her little pot for her. Queer-colored flames she makes under it, from plants she gathers on top of the cliff at the full moon——"

"Does the priest know what she's up to?" Sarah asked.

"No, he does not, then, for no one has the courage to tell him."

"Do the neighbors know?"

"She's a disgrace to me always," said Morgan. "They know she's a miser with the money and they know she'd only have me marry a girl with a big fortune. But I'd have married you, Sarah, fortune or no. You were a fine girl that time, when you were young and good-looking."

None of us spoke now for we could see that Sarah had some knack of getting Morgan to say things that he had been trying for years to hide from the world.

"I know what the people do be saying about me, Sarah— that I have no spirit, that I should have found a girl years ago and brought her home. But how could I bring her home to that house, and that old woman all day planning devilment, until maybe she'd drive the poor girl daft with her plotting and I out in the fields? Could I put my own mother out of the house, onto the side of the road? Could I go off to the New World and leave her alone? My father was the lucky one—he died young."

"Do you think the neighbors know she makes spells and says her little rhymes?"

"They know it, all right, for I overheard them talking about it. They think like yourself that she's just a silly old woman, though they don't like it. They never come in to visit her and have a cup of tea with her, the way they do with each other. They're afraid she'd grudge them the tea, too. And she knows what they're thinking about—she often told me, when I'd listen to her, which isn't often because I don't like that kind of talk. She has a bad story about every one of our neighbors. It's no wonder they won't come near her."

Colman had got his courage back. Now he piped up from the hob:

"Two wrongs don't make a right. You had no business to

be coming around here robbing and murdering, even if your mother is an old disgrace——"

There was no profit in this kind of talk. I interrupted:

"The red-haired woman was not a ghost, anyway. I'll swear she will turn out to be my aunt Maggie."

Morgan flashed around on me, his eyes full of venom.

"You're making game of me."

He made a threatening move toward me. I said:

"I am not making game of you. My aunt Maggie has red hair. She can sail a hooker, better than any man I ever saw. If she was around this part of the world, she was looking for us and for the *Santa Maria,* our boat, that she helped to build."

"A woman to build a boat! I don't believe it."

"Wait till you meet Maggie. There's nothing she couldn't do."

"Why would she be looking for you?"

"Because Ciarán brought her a message that we're alive, when everyone thought we were dead. She may have found out what place he came from, though he didn't tell her. If she even guessed at it, she would come around looking for us."

"Why didn't Ciarán tell her where he came from? Why did everyone think you were dead?"

"We wanted to sail to Spain to bring Sarah home to her father. We knew that if we told anyone about it, we wouldn't be let go. It's a long story," I said impatiently. "Where exactly was Maggie when you saw her last?"

"She was about halfway between Inishownan and Flaherty's Island. She was heading south."

"Did you hail her?"

"Hail her! I'd as soon hail the devil—begging your pardon, if she is your aunt Maggie." A faintly humorous look had crept into his eyes. "I'll be the first to help you to find her now and the first to leg it if she turns out to be what I think she is."

163

"You don't think it any more, or you wouldn't say that," Sarah said.

"I suppose I don't, Sarah," said Morgan. "Bit by bit I'd be getting sense if I had you to talk to sometimes."

But a second later he gave a long wailing squeal and shot across the kitchen to the far wall. There he half-crouched, half-stood, with his arms and legs splayed out, seeming by his wriggling movements to be trying to work his way backwards through the wall. That squeal had gone through us all like a red-hot knife. Sarah turned white. Tomás whipped a long-blade knife out of his pocket in an instinctive movement, so fast that its blade flashed like a light. Juan leaped to stand by his father's shoulder. The rest of us just seemed to be turned to stone.

Our eyes had darted at once to the door, following Morgan's look of horror. It was the usual kind of door that we have, a full inner door which stood open and a half-door which was closed, so that it was like having a big unglazed window in the kitchen.

Now, when we looked, framed in the dark space above the half-door was Maggie. I must admit that she looked a bit wild. Her red hair, which was wispy at the best of times, stuck out around her head like a halo, blown and tangled by the wind. Her black shawl hung half off her shoulders, and the neck of her blouse was pulled awry. Her hands resting on the top of the door were red from the ropes that she had been hauling all day, and her face was red too, from the salty winds. She looked fiercely, quickly into every face that was turned toward her, until her eyes rested on me. Then she slid back the bolt of the door and strode into the kitchen.

I rushed toward her.

"Maggie, Maggie! How did you get here?"

"I borrowed your father's boat. I told him I'd go and find you, alive or dead."

"Dead! Don't they believe we're alive?"

164

"How can they believe what they don't see? They had your wake before the boy brought word that you were safe. That's the only reason why they're not having one now."

"How did you find us?" I asked, putting away the other complications for the moment.

"I didn't find you," Maggie said. "I found the *Santa Maria*."

While we were having this conversation, I was aware that the others in the company were recovering their senses. Tomás had turned a little aside and was rather furtively putting away his knife. Morgan was detaching himself gradually from the wall and looking foolish, as well he might. As Sarah took a step forward to welcome Maggie, old Colman sprang past her with his hands out and hooted:

"Come in, come in, you valiant woman! You're as welcome as the flowers of May. The boys here told me how you took over the building of the *Santa Maria* and made her fit to sail the seven seas. Sarah! Have we e'er a drop in the bottle till we drink her health? There isn't her like in all Ireland."

Maggie was eyeing Colman as if he were crazy. He looked it, indeed, in his ragged clothes and with his five-day beard. Her habit of silence saved her from asking me directly what kind of mad company I had found. She let Sarah lead her over to the big chair by the fire and place a glass of poiteen in her hand. Sarah poured some for Colman and Tomás too, and a little for herself. The last one she filled was for Morgan and as she handed it to him she said:

"When you drink with us, Morgan, you'll have to be our friend afterwards."

He did not answer, but when Colman bawled out his toast to Maggie, the finest woman in the five kingdoms of Ireland, Morgan took a drink from his glass too. No one, of course, gave a drop to us. Sarah poured goat's milk for us after a while and we made a show of drinking it, but I had already

made a private vow to have done with goat's milk from the day I would get home to Rossmore.

Though I was burning with curiosity, still I held off questioning Maggie further until I could see that her drink had warmed her up. Then I began on her again:

"How did you find the *Santa Maria*, Maggie?"

"By chance," she said. "I was giving up hope. For all I knew, it was in Galway I should be searching, or in Ballyvaughan over the far side of the Bay. The only thing I had in the way of news was that on the day that boy came to Rossmore, someone saw a strange horse tethered in a field above near the cross."

"God bless their eyesight," said Ciarán sourly. "They don't miss much."

"And that person thought it might be a Carraroe horse," Maggie said. "I didn't put much trust in that, for how can you tell a Carraroe horse from a Rossmore horse? Anyway I came up to John's father and I told him I had an idea where you might be. I asked him to come with me, but he wouldn't. He would have gone alone, all right, but he wouldn't go with me for fear I'd bring him bad luck, though he's my own brother. To give him his due, John, it was your mother said that, and your father wouldn't go against her. He gave me the boat, though. That was something. In the dark of the morning I sailed out from Rossmore and I'm combing this part of the world since daylight."

"You found the *Santa Maria* in the dark."

" 'Twas the trawler I saw. It has a light on the masthead."

"A light?"

"I lit it when we were leaving the boats," Tomás said. "I always do that, even in daylight, in case I wouldn't be back before dark."

"I sailed in behind it and the next thing I saw was my own *Santa Maria* tied up behind it. I was delighted with that until I saw the cats."

"What cats?"

"Five or six tabby cats, big and small. They frightened the wits out of me—they were dancing around on the *Santa Maria*——"

"Dancing?"

"Playing, I suppose they were, but the first sight of them, they looked as if they were dancing. You know they say cats on a boat are a sign of bad luck."

I turned to Morgan and said:

"Do you hear that? Did you ever hear of a ghost or a spirit to be worrying about bad luck?"

"Hold your whisht," said Morgan with a sheepish look at Maggie.

"That boat has had so much bad luck, it should be sunk seven times over," Maggie said, and she laughed. "That's the way I worked it out. If anyone can go near that boat with the cats on it, I said to myself, it's a red-haired woman. So I went over and I pish-wished to them, and over they came to me. Then I saw that they were fat house cats and I said to them: 'Let ye come off that boat, now, and lead me up to your own house.' They wouldn't stir at first, until I started up the road. I called them then, and they all came along with me. They ran all around me and in front of me until they led me up here."

"Why wouldn't they know the way?" said Colman. "They're my own cats. And would you believe me, I never thought of them since I got home."

"Were you in Galway?" Maggie asked doubtfully, obviously thinking what a scarecrow he would have looked in the city.

"No, I was in another place," Colman said with surprising discretion. "There was no one here to feed the cats. It was the smell of the fish that drew them to the boats, I suppose."

I had not thought of the cats either, though they had been in every corner of the house before we left for Spain. Now the mother cat sprang into the kitchen across the half-door. Outside we could hear the kittens mewing. I opened the door and they all came trooping in.

"They're fine cats," Maggie said in admiration. "There's nothing makes a house look so comfortable as a fat cat."

"I like cats too," said Morgan, "but my mother doesn't want any of them, for fear they would be watching her up to her tricks, I suppose."

Maggie turned around to take a long look at Morgan. Then she gave a hoot of laughter and said:

"You're a big boy now to be minding what your mother says. If you want a cat, why don't you have one?"

"There's a woman that would stand up to your mother, Morgan," Sarah said softly.

The others were chuckling and no one heard her but myself. It put a queer idea into my head. Maggie seemed to have changed completely since I had seen her last. I had certainly never thought to see her sitting in a room full of strangers, chatting and joking. The worried look that she had worn as long as I had known her was gone, and it was not hard to guess at the reason for it. Our mission had been a success. Her father's boat had sailed to Flaherty's Island. Now suddenly I realized that she did not know the rest of our story.

"Maggie," I said, "we haven't told you yet that we sailed to Spain in the *Santa Maria*."

"You did! On the trawler! So that's where you were, and the whole parish crying after you. And tell me now, is Spain a fine country?"

"Maggie, we sailed to Spain on our *Santa Maria*, the hooker—not the trawler."

This time she took it in. Her eyes widened with astonishment and delight. Her grip tightened on her glass, which had seemed for a moment to be about to slip to the floor.

"Is it true? Did they sail to Spain?" she asked the company in general.

"They did, faith," said Colman, "and they brought back my daughter Sarah that I hadn't seen for twenty years and never thought to see again in life."

"You did that? Our *Santa Maria* did that?"

"She's a perfect boat, for sure, Maggie," I said. "She weathered the storm on the way here like a bird, and out in the Bay of Biscay a squall stood her on her beam ends and she never thought of sinking."

"Thanks and glory be to God," said Maggie and she almost sang it. "My father was right. Wait till they hear of this in Rossmore!"

Jim and I exchanged looks which said quite clearly that there might be no need to mention how we had come to land on Flaherty's Island in the first place. Perhaps at some future time, if Maggie happened to see the repair of the boat at low tide, we might make some explanations. Fortunately there was no great hurry with it.

Colman stood up briskly and said:

"For five nights past I've been dreaming of going to sleep with a stomach full of *brochán*. Now if it's all the same to the company, I'll make a pot of it and we'll all have some."

"Why didn't they give you your *brochán* for five nights?" Maggie asked.

"They don't serve it in that place, ever," Colman said. "Redden up the fire, there, Sarah! We'll show these Spaniards something."

"Sarah sometimes makes it at home," Tomás said.

"She does! Well, mine will be better."

Better or worse, it made me so sleepy that I began to see the room through a fog. Several times I was thinking of moving into the vacant hob and putting my head back and falling asleep. The lamp glowed and the flames of the fire flickered, and the talk hummed in my head. Sarah and Morgan had a long conversation with each other and seemed very friendly.

At last they were all standing up and arguing about where

we were to sleep. Maggie was to have the settle bed in the kitchen. Since we had never got around to bringing up our bedding, we were to sleep on the boats, except for Sarah and Tomás who were to have Sarah's old room.

"I kept it just as you left it, Sarah," Colman said, opening the door and holding the lamp proudly high for her to look in.

"You did, Father," she said.

I saw her eye travel with amusement from the gray bedspread to the gray curtains.

"It's dry as a bone," he assured her eagerly.

While this was going on, I saw Morgan slip out of the kitchen. A good riddance, I thought. None of us would have wanted to walk down to the beach with him, after the way we had captured him there. I wondered if I would ever see him again.

All four of us slept on the trawler that night. There were six bunks, and we used the four lower ones. As we got into them, it occurred to me that it would not be too difficult to build a couple into the *Santa Maria*. If we were to do this, she would be the first Connemara hooker ever to have such a stylish fitting.

My dream of sleeping on a featherbed that night did not come true after all. However, the mattresses of the bunks were filled with something softer than our spiky straw, and the gentle movement of the little ship soon sent us to sleep.

(11)

When we came up on deck the next morning, it was broad
daylight. The sun warmed the planks of the deck under our
feet. It was good to see the little harbor full of boats. My
father's hooker was moored behind the trawler, where
Maggie had left it last night. It brought me suddenly to think
of my parents, and to wish I might see them soon again.

I looked over the trawler's side and saw that the water of
the little fjord was thick with bladderwrack. I called out to
the others:

"The weed is in! Come on!"

This was enough for us Connemara boys. In two seconds
our clothes were off and we were jumping like fish into the
sea. It was silky smooth and full of the wild exciting smell of
autumn. Juan followed us more slowly, lowering himself
shivering into the water, watching our splashing with a careful eye.

"Come on down where it's warm," we urged him. "When
the weed is in, the Atlantic Ocean warms up."

"Warm!" he said. "When I saw you in there, I thought it
must be so, but it's like snow."

All the same he seemed to enjoy the swim, and we crawled
up the rocks in a few minutes glowing all over and dancing

about to dry ourselves in the sun. When we were dressed, we ran all the way up to the house.

As we approached it, we saw an astonishing sight. Every wall and bush in its vicinity was draped with washing—sheets, curtains, clothing of all kinds. Outside the front door, Maggie had the washtub on a creepie stool and was scrubbing and pounding at more things.

Sarah gave us breakfast. There was no sign of Colman.

"He's off with the pigs' feed," Sarah said.

He came in a few minutes later, looking exactly as he had done when we saw him first, in spite of his five nights in the cold of the ruined schoolhouse. Even his voice had not suffered much. It was still the same cracked old woman's voice.

"There ye are at last!" he bawled at us. "I'd have rousted ye out long ago only Sarah wouldn't let me. Tell me, now, isn't it a grand thing to have a few women around the house? Did ye see Maggie outside? Doesn't Sarah look fine there at my kitchen table, making my bread for me?"

"She does, faith," said Ciarán.

Tomás came out of the inner room.

"But she belongs to me," he said calmly. "We'll be getting you another one to stand where she is. Of course we'll be coming from time to time to see how you're doing."

"Another one? What other one? I don't want another one."

"Mary."

Colman drew himself up like a pouting turkey cock. Before he could speak. Tomás went on:

"There will be an end of all this quarreling. I never had it in my family and I'm not going to have it now. You are the cause of it all. Neither Sarah nor Mary wants to quarrel."

"Your family! Your family!" Colman stuttered.

"We are all one family now," Tomás said. "All your sons in America too, though I have never seen them. It will take you no more than five minutes to forget all the years that are lost. It will be very easy, because in all those years Mary never said a bitter word to you. Isn't that true? It was you that sent her those dreadful messages, but she never sent any of the same kind back to you. She told the priest to tell you to come and stay with her and she would care for you. Isn't that true?"

"Was that a message from Mary?" Colman asked in a small, meek voice, like a grandfather rat.

"Of course it was. Do you think the priest would have thought of it himself? When you see her——"

Instantly he flared up again.

"I won't go to Inishownan! I won't be a laughingstock for everyone, to see me crawling to my own daughter——"

"You won't have to go to Inishownan. Mary will come to you."

"How do you know? Maybe she'll refuse, same as I did."

"Mary has no stupid pride. I know her well."

"You know her!"

"Yes. She is one of my oldest friends. You always knew that. I land on Inishownan for a few hours whenever I am in this neighborhood."

"Did Sarah——" He paused and a look of agony came over his face. "Did Sarah land on Inishownan sometimes, too?"

"Never," Tomás said. "She has never come to Ireland since she left it with me."

We held our breath, you may be sure, during this conversation. When Tomás said that Mary had no stupid pride, I measured the distance to the door, thinking that now the sparks would surely fly and that all sensible people should be out of danger. But Tomás had a way of continually forcing Colman's interest on to new things, so that he seemed almost to forget to rage and shout. Later, when we were by ourselves, I said to Ciarán that it was a pity Tomás had not said some of those things to Colman twenty years before.

"He was younger then," Ciarán said. "He wouldn't have had the power he has now. And Sarah would have preferred to take the easy way, knowing what an old rasper her father was. Don't forget, Colman was twenty years younger too."

Throughout the morning, Jim and I lived in terror of being left alone with Colman while the rest of the party would go over to Inishownan.

"We have no reason to go," Jim said. "We have no business with them since we're not even cousins. The old fellow will be like a bag of fleas when they're gone. We'll never be able to keep him quiet."

In the end, it was Ciarán who stayed. He fixed a calm eye on Colman and said in his soft drawl:

"We'll be talking about the painting I promised to do for him, and the bit of thatching. I said I'd stay with him a while. One of these days I'll go over to see my grandmother and fix it with her."

"And we can be talking over what you'll say to her," said Colman. "She'll have her ear stretched long for a good story that she can be spreading all over Connacht ever after."

We went to Inishownan on the trawler. Maggie came too, to have a look at the big world, she said. She seemed to have become very fond of Sarah and stayed close by her throughout the journey.

We had been longing to see Inishownan, because of hearing so much about it. It was bigger than Colman's island, of course, and had a good population. I wondered why the people had not all gone away to America too.

"It was the pier that kept them," Sarah said. "All winter long, when you couldn't get off or onto our island, the pilot boat and the lifeboat would be able to call at Inishownan. The Spaniards came in, and the man from Brittany for the lobsters. The boats were safe there, so that if there was a storm sometimes they'd have grand company for a few days."

Maggie said:

" 'Twas lonesome for a young girl, alone with no one but her father on Flaherty's Island."

"It was the back of beyond," said Sarah. "People didn't come visiting us because if you landed and the wind came up, you might have to stay a week."

She would not have said it, but we were all thinking that a week under Colman's roof when he was in his heyday would have been a trial of anyone's strength.

Tomás obviously knew the waters around Inishownan very well. As he brought us in, Maggie became very silent. I was disappointed at this. I had been delighted at her new liveliness and had hoped never again to see that look of anxiety that she had always worn at home. I supposed it had become such a habit with her that she could not change it all at once. Then I saw that she was nervous, and I thought it was at the prospect of meeting strangers.

Sure enough, when we landed at the quay she seemed to want to hide herself in the middle of our group. It was a short, wide quay with a curve at the tip. A few hookers were moored there, and I could see that lobster fishing was their main business. There were lobster pots everywhere—on the boats and on the quay. Since it was dinnertime, there was no one about.

The quay was at a sheltered part of the island, which rose up to a low hill with an old fort on top, like the ones you see in Aran. At either side there were flat rocks, worn smooth by the sea. Above that we could see good green fields with cattle and horses grazing.

"It's a fine place," Maggie said. "Fine land and grand, healthy beasts."

"Grand people too, Maggie," Tomás said. "They work hard and spare their money, but they'd give you the shirt off their back all the same."

"All except Morgan's mother," said Maggie dryly.

"She's a silly old thing," Tomás said. "We won't be long fixing her. The people should have put a stop to her games long ago, but I suppose they didn't like to interfere."

A fine wide road led up from the quay to where we could see a group of houses. Sarah was impatient to be off, but of course we had to wait until the trawler was securely moored by Tomás and Juan. Then we started up the road. Sarah walked close by her husband, with her shawl pulled tightly around her head. With Maggie crowding in behind, they looked like a group of explorers just landed in doubtful territory. The three of us stayed a little back from them but we did not talk.

The first house we came to was right by the road, separated from it only by a little dusty patch of ground crisscrossed by the claws of hens. The sound of our feet brought an old woman trotting to the door. When she saw us, she gave a little shriek of delight and came running out.

"Tomás! You're a sight for sore eyes! Welcome and twenty welcomes! When did you come?"

"This minute," said Tomás, gesturing toward the quay where the trawler could just be seen.

"And how are they all at home?" The old woman's eyes sparkled with curiosity as they ran from one of us to the other.

"They're fine, Katta, fine," said Tomás. "I have some of them with me this time. You remember Sarah, of course."

Katta gave a louder shriek and fell on Sarah as women do, wrapping her arms around her and rocking her about as she hugged and kissed her.

"Sareen, you're as handsome as ever, so you are. And are these your sons, God bless them?"

Juan was pointed out to her and she fell on him too. She didn't do anything to me nor to Jim though we had braced ourselves for it. Maggie was spared too. Tomás said:

"We're going up to visit Mary. We spent last night with Colman Flaherty and we're bringing Mary over with us now, to visit her father. These boys sailed over to Spain in their hooker to ask Sarah to come and see her family. Maggie is our good friend from Rossmore. She built the hooker they sailed in, or a great part of it at least."

I thought the old woman would explode as she took in this tremendous collection of news bit by bit. She was quite unable to reply, except to say over and over:

"Well, isn't it the sport! Isn't it the great sport!"

Tomás led us on, chuckling and saying:

"That will settle a lot of things. She'll send the story into every house in the island, as good as the radio and nearly as fast."

Not far from Katta's, we turned up a short road that ended at Mary's house. Mary was a tall, straight woman, many years older than Sarah but still very handsome. She was serving dinner to her husband and family, who were all gathered around the kitchen table. When we crowded in the doorway, she looked at us in silence for a moment, and then turned very carefully to lay the potato basket safely on the table before running to her sister.

Jim and I backed quietly out into the yard.

"The *Santa Maria* did good work," I said softly. "There's no one will say a word against her ever again, after this."

Presently Tomás appeared at the door to conduct us inside. We were praised and fed until we felt like a couple of favorite cats. A queer thing I discovered that day, however, was that one gets tired of hearing oneself praised, in time. One doesn't get tired of being thought a hero, just of listening to people say it over and over.

Mary had three sons, handsome big men rather like Sarah's, and a daughter of our age. She was a quiet girl, who went about the kitchen with her eyes down doing all kinds of work for her mother. Very soon the neighbors began to come in to have a look at us and tell us we were as brave as Ulysses, and to drink our health. When this had been going on for a while, and we were lapping it up like cats, I chanced to look over at the girl who was rinsing glasses in a dish by the back

door. Her hair was tied up with a big white ribbon and it fell in curls around her face, but I could see that she was smiling to herself. Then she lifted her head for a second and looked straight at me, her eyes dancing and her mouth working with the effort of not laughing aloud.

Seconds later I was outside, cooling my hot face in the

breeze. No one missed me except Jim, who came out a
moment later. We sat on the low stone wall in front of the
house while people passed in and out, until it seemed certain
that everyone on the island must have had a look at Sarah.
Katta was one of the last to arrive. She looked tired, almost as

if she should have had her tongue hanging out like a sheep dog that has put in a hard day's work rounding up sheep.

Suddenly Jim said:

"Here comes Morgan MacDonagh. Let's run."

But it was too late. Morgan had seen us. If we moved away now, it would be clear to him that we had not wanted to speak to him. We had parted on such friendly terms that this would have been all the more uncivil. Besides, he looked different today. His back was straighter and his eyes had lost something of their brooding, bitter look. The effect of this was to make him seem much younger than he had done before. He came over to us and said:

"Welcome to Inishownan. Is Maggie inside?"

"Yes, she came with us," I said, surprised at the question.

"Go in and fetch her out for me like a good boy."

I got down off the wall. Immediately Morgan sat in my place and began to chat with Jim about our trip to Spain, as if we had never knocked him down and sat on him in our lives.

I edged into the kitchen. The men and the old women had got their pipes going and the air was blue with smoke. I saw at once where Maggie was, near the door. Katta was talking to her, rattling along like a threshing engine without ever a pause. I leaned down to Maggie's ear and whispered:

"Morgan MacDonagh is outside. He wants to speak to you."

She stood up immediately and came with me. Katta never ceased from her talk. She just turned her head the other way and addressed it all to the woman at her other side.

Morgan said to Maggie:

"Welcome to Inishownan."

Then he took her arm and led her up the road away from the quay, talking earnestly to her all the time.

Jim said after a moment:

"The world is surely coming to an end. Do you see what I see?"

"I don't know what I see," I said. "How are we going to live a quiet life in Rossmore after this?"

"It won't ever be too quiet again. For one thing, we'll have a lot of visiting to do, and maybe a lot of visitors coming to us as well."

Presently we went inside to see if the party were going to go on all day. Tomás caught my eye and came weaving through the crowded room to say:

"We'll be going soon. We have just one more thing to do. Did Morgan come?"

"A few minutes ago. He asked me to fetch out Maggie to him. They're gone up the road together. What's going on, I'd like to know."

"Can't you guess?" He turned back and called out to Sarah: "Time to be going. Is Mary ready?"

She was, and a moment later they were all outside. But only Mary's husband went directly to the quay. Tomás turned up the hill, walking between Mary and Sarah. They walked fast, and this time we did not hang back. Something warned me that if we did not stay close, we might find ourselves excluded from the next part of the business. When we saw the three of them march firmly into a house at the top of the village, a little away from the other houses, we waited for no invitation but walked right in after them.

It was a fine house. That morning I did not notice everything about it because I was busy listening to the talk, but later I came to know it very well indeed. It had a bigger kitchen than we usually have, and fine solid furniture of the kind that could be handed on from father to son for hundreds of years. There was a range of jugs and bowls on the tall dresser, all blue and gold—the most beautiful I had ever seen. There was a big wall clock with weights and chains, and a dash churn, and a whole family of cooking pots, big and small, so that you could always find one that was just the right size.

Such a beautiful kitchen should have been any woman's pride, you would think, but dust and ashes lay thick on everything. The crockery on the dresser was veiled in dust, and there was dust on the rounded sides of all the pots except one, so that you could see they were never used. I had time only to notice this before the old woman who was crouched on the hob stood up and faced us. Before she had time to speak, Mary said:

"Mrs. MacDonagh, I brought Sarah to visit you, when you didn't come down to the house. Maybe Katta didn't tell you; she's home from Spain after twenty years, and this is her husband Tomás, and that's her son Juan. And these are the Rossmore boys that sailed over to fetch her."

The old woman glowered at us. Then she said grudgingly:

"You're welcome, Sarah. I knew you were below at Mary's but the legs are bad with me and I couldn't go down."

"I'm glad to see you, ma'am," Sarah said gently. "My father is getting old and I'll be coming sometimes to see him, and over to visit Mary. That way I'll be able to come up here from time to time."

" 'Tis here in this house you should be living," the old woman shouted suddenly, like an old crow on a wall. "And your sons should be my grandsons. That useless son of mine was never able to bring home a wife like you—a wife that you could trust, with a good brain in her head and a good pair of hands on her, and a mouth that she could keep shut at times. They don't make women like that any more."

"Maybe he thought you wouldn't welcome his wife," Mary said.

"Of course I'd welcome her. Sure, you can see how my house is a show to the world and I not able to clean it. The legs are bad with me. Every time Morgan comes in that door don't I be telling him he's no good not to have found himself a wife like every other man, with a bit of land or something in her stocking—a sparing, crafty kind of a girl that you could be fond of."

Jim and I looked at each other in silent delight at this description of the desirable things in a wife. Sarah said:

"Maybe you said too much. Maybe you frightened him."

"He's no man to be frightened so easy," the old woman said with contempt. Her voice took on a sly note which went strangely with its coarse quality. "But I have new ways that are old ways too, for getting him a wife. One of these days he'll walk into this house with her, you'll see."

Tomás stepped quickly forward and said:

"That will happen today. Morgan has found a wife."

"But the full moon is not till Friday. It had to be a Friday full moon."

The old woman turned the color of the ashes on her dead hearth—a queer, brownish yellow. Slowly she sank back into the chimney corner and leaned her head against the wall. Mary darted across to hold her, calling out:

"Quick, look in the press. See is there a bottle of something there——"

I was the nearest to the dresser. I wrenched the doors open and saw a bottle of poiteen half full. I took it out and poured some into a mug off the shelf above, noticing as I did so that the bottle was thick with dust. Whatever the old woman's vices were, drinking poiteen was not one of them.

She revived after a mouthful or two of it, and sat up straighter, but she did not attempt to stand up. I remember that I felt no trace of pity for her, even now, because her wicked tongue had driven Morgan to such lengths. Believe it or not, I still had not guessed the plan that had been composed since yesterday. It was not until Morgan came into the kitchen with Maggie beside him, held firmly by the arm, that I knew she was the wife of whom Tomás had spoken.

Morgan and his mother looked at each other for a full half-minute. Tomás said:

"Go on, Morgan."

"This is Maggie Hernon from Rossmore, that's going to be my wife," Morgan said loudly. He hesitated and seemed to pull his wits about him by force. Then he went on: "She'll go home to her own place today and next week I'll follow her and we'll be married." He stopped again and then said with a grin: "Say a welcome to her, Mother. It's a wonder I got a woman to take me at all, at this hour of my life, let alone a fine woman like Maggie."

"You are welcome."

The old woman said the words in a half whisper. Maggie took Morgan's hand off her arm and went across to her.

"Thank you for that word," she said. "I'll mind your house for you and do every little thing for yourself, and with God's help we'll have good times."

It seemed to us fair to claim getting a wife for Morgan as yet another of the *Santa Maria*'s good deeds. All the time while we were in that house, Mrs. MacDonagh never took her eyes off Maggie. Long afterwards Tomás told me that she thought she had manufactured Maggie with one of her spells. Maggie's red hair was taken as proof of this. One good effect of it was that she always treated Maggie with great respect, and another was that she gave up her attempts at spell-weaving for fear of what she might produce the next time.

I had a few scruples about handing Maggie over to Morgan, but she seemed very pleased with the business so there was nothing to be said. Already they were planning to build a new hooker on the pattern of the *Santa Maria*. Since our trip to Spain, Morgan said, people would say it was good luck and not bad that Maggie brought to boats and sailors. This was how it turned out to be.

Morgan did not come back to Flaherty's Island with us. We were all glad when he said he would not come. Indeed I thought it would be a good thing if he were never to set foot on that island again, after the things he had done there and the way he had coveted it. Probably Maggie would see to it that he stayed away, I thought. But I never knew afterwards whether she heard the whole story of his doings there.

Mary's three sons were on the trawler with their father when we reached it. They were delighted with Juan and from their talk I forecast that the trawler was going to run a passenger service between Commillas and the islands for the next few years.

It was strange to repeat the pattern of yesterday's events. Again we landed in the little natural harbor and waited impatiently while the trawler was made fast. Again we walked up the grass-grown road, a bigger group this time. Again the quietness of the island seemed to have something threatening in it, though the evening sun turned the standing barley to gold.

As we approached the house, I felt a choking in my chest, a terror of an empty house waiting for us, with a cold hearth. No one spoke a word.

Then suddenly I knew what to do. I darted out from the back of our group and ran like a bird up the lane, calling out at the top of my voice, breaking the terrible silence into a thousand pieces:

"Colman! Colman! Here comes your family—grandsons, sons-in-law, daughters and all. Come on out!"

I heard a chair turn over inside the house and first Ciarán and then Colman appeared at the door.

Colman took one astonished look at the group and then he came bounding out to greet them. It seemed as if in that moment he forgot all the grievances that had soured his life. His eyes darted from his daughters to his grandsons and back again, not knowing which gave him the most pleasure. Neither Mary nor Sarah showed the smallest sign that they remembered the terrible things that he had said in the past.

187

Naturally no one mentioned that Maggie was going to marry Morgan. I pulled Ciarán outside after a while to break this news to him. He doubled up with laughter.

"It would be a pity to spoil two houses with them," he said and added quickly: "But Maggie is too goodhearted for him. Perhaps she'll improve him a bit."

I did not know what to say, since I was fond of Maggie. All I could answer was:

"I think Morgan and his mother have met their match."

We slept that night on the trawler again and the next morning we sailed for home. This time Maggie sailed the *Santa Maria* and Jim and I took my father's boat. Though Maggie had told me that the *Santa Maria* was to belong to me, still I felt a black jealousy at seeing Maggie move gradually away and away ahead of us toward home. She never turned her head, nor looked back at the shore where old Colman and Sarah and Ciarán and Juan and Tomás stood waving to us and wishing us luck. Watching her expertly haul up sail and then sit like a statue at the helm, I thought it was no wonder that Morgan had believed she was a creature from another world.

It had been decided that Sarah would stay with her father for a while. Tomás and Juan were to go home to Commillas. Ciarán had wanted to come with us, to see the sensation that would be caused by our arrival home, but he was persuaded to stay with Colman too. The excitement of the last weeks had left the old man very nervous. The morning we left, through the open door we had all heard him talking to the goats as he milked them, telling them to be civil to Sarah:

"With a woman around the house, we must all mend our manners. 'Twon't be hard for ye—she's quiet and easy as she always was. She's gone a long time—a long, long time."

Maggie reached Rossmore a good hour ahead of us. A natural result of this was that when we got to the quay, the whole townland was there to watch us land. Remembering

Mary's daughter, the girl who had been laughing at us over the washing-up, I tried not to puff out my chest and walk up to our house like a conquering general. It would have been easy to have done it, for the air was full of murmured praise and astonishment at our exploit. Jim's great-grandfather who had sailed the Atlantic with Captain Hennessy was given credit for handing on his skill. Maggie and myself had to get our credit direct, and it was said many times that our daring and our enterprise would be talked about over the winter fires in Rossmore for hundreds of years to come.

Our parents gave us the welcome that you give to someone who has returned from the grave. For days after we came back, my mother wanted to have me always within sight. When I was in bed at night, several times I awoke to find her standing over me with a candle in her hand. Jim told me that his mother was the same.

You can imagine, therefore, after we had been a week at home, the howl that went up when we said that we had promised to visit Flaherty's Island again. I think we should never have been allowed to go, if it had not been as an escort for Maggie when she sailed to Inishownan with Morgan on her wedding day.

That wedding was a sensation in Rossmore and in the townlands around it. Everyone knew Maggie because of her house being beside the quay. On the days before her marriage, it seemed that someone was on the doorstep every hour with a present for her. Wonderful and useful presents they were too—a roll of butter in a cabbage leaf, a hen, a clutch of eggs, a squealing young pig in a sack, a china dog to ornament the mantelpiece, a dish that someone's great-grandmother had bought in Galway on her honeymoon. And she got five alarm clocks with shining bells on them. I was there when she opened the parcel containing the fifth one. She laughed until she was quite helpless, rocking up and down in her chair.

"Five alarm clocks!" she said at last. "What will I do with them all? I'll have one for every room in the house and two over."

"The two over will do for wedding presents in the years to come," I suggested.

"Such good neighbors I have," she said. "I'll tell you a queer thing: there was a time when I hated every one of them, thinking they cared nothing for me, that they wouldn't walk into my house to talk to me as they did to everyone else. But now I'm thinking 'twas I made them that way, from being so watchful. Promise me one thing, John, that as long as you live you'll always keep the house door standing open to your neighbors."

Since I have always loved visitors and company and talk and stories, I made her that promise. I have never had any trouble in keeping it.